Falling for the Mom-to-Be

Jenna Mindel

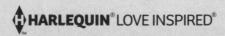

HARLEQUIN® LOVE INSPIRED®

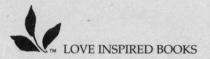 LOVE INSPIRED BOOKS

Recycling programs for this product may not exist in your area.

ISBN-13: 978-0-373-87982-3

Falling for the Mom-to-Be

Copyright © 2015 by Jenna Mindel

All rights reserved. Except for use in any review, the reproduction or utilization of this work in whole or in part in any form by any electronic, mechanical or other means, now known or hereinafter invented, including xerography, photocopying and recording, or in any information storage or retrieval system, is forbidden without the written permission of the editorial office, Love Inspired Books, 233 Broadway, New York, NY 10279 U.S.A.

This is a work of fiction. Names, characters, places and incidents are either the product of the author's imagination or are used fictitiously, and any resemblance to actual persons, living or dead, business establishments, events or locales is entirely coincidental.

This edition published by arrangement with Love Inspired Books.

® and TM are trademarks of Love Inspired Books, used under license. Trademarks indicated with ® are registered in the United States Patent. and Trademark Office, the Canadian Intellectual Property Office and in other countries.

www.Harlequin.com

Printed in U.S.A.

Blessed are those who mourn,
for they will be comforted.
—*Matthew* 5:4

A huge thank-you to Doug LaLonde
for answering my many questions about
freighters and shipping on the Great Lakes.
You guys are rock stars out there!

Prologue

March

Annie Marshall stood in the middle of the produce section of a big chain grocery store the next town over from her own. People passed by her without a nod or glance. They didn't know her. And that was good. Too many knew her in Maple Springs. If she'd have gone to the corner IGA, she'd have been showered with words of sympathy and pitiful looks.

Tonight, she wasn't in the mood.

Annie had broken free from her house that was shrouded with whispers and mourning and did something normal people do. She went grocery shopping. She wanted freedom from her sister and their aunt and their careless coddling. Freedom from their compulsive comfort given to compensate for the geographic and emotional distance between them.

Tonight, she was mad.

Mad at God for taking her husband of fifteen years with a sudden heart attack, out of the blue. Mad at her aunt and sister for treating her like spun glass, ready to break. Mad at Jack for not taking better care of himself.

He'd never come home again.

Jack...

Her throat tightened, so she closed her eyes and counted.

Annie always counted when on the edge of losing it. It had started when she was a kid because her mom refused to let her throw tantrums. It came in handy when she'd received word of her parents' death while in college. Her sister, barely high-school-aged, went to live with their aunt. Life went on.

And Annie had been counting since Jack's funeral. A week ago? It seemed like years.

She felt a touch to her shoulder and spun.

"Hey." Matthew Zelinsky searched her face. His blue eyes were dark with concern. "What are you doing over here?"

Annie's throat went dry. "Shopping. What about you?"

"Same." He shrugged as he glanced at her empty cart save for a bunch of bananas. Jack had loved bananas.

Matthew placed his empty basket on the floor and then lifted her bundle of fruit and put it back on the shelf. He took her by the hand. "Come on."

Annie didn't argue. She followed him outside into the cold, damp night. Snow banks still loomed high in the parking lot but had melted some from the day's rain. Dirt and silt covered their tops. Thin layers of ice shone in the overhead lights where puddles had been. The end of March wasn't pretty in northern Michigan.

Her breath blew cold smoke in front of her. "I saw you at the funeral, but you were gone before I could even talk to you."

"I know. I'm sorry."

He opened the passenger side of his pickup truck for her and she climbed in. The truck was big and loaded.

Jack had gone with him at the end of January to pick it out. Off-season.

Matthew got in, started the engine and cranked up the heat.

She leaned back against the plush seats and sighed. "Nice truck. Do you like it?"

"Yeah, it's great." He turned toward her. "How are you?"

She shrugged, knowing she couldn't put on a grand performance with Matthew. He knew her too well. "How am I supposed to be?"

"I don't know." He gave her a slanted smile. "If you figure it out, let me know."

They sat in silence a moment. The only noise was the whirl of the heater. Matthew reached for her hand and she held on. There wasn't anything either of them could say to make it better or worse. They both loved Jack. And now he was gone.

"I'm heading out in the morning."

Annie felt another stab of loss.

Matthew was Jack's best friend and first mate on a Great Lakes freighter where they'd worked together for years. Matthew had been the one to find Jack dead in his cabin after they'd been on the lakes only a week into the shipping season. Their freighter had loaded up at the calcite plant in Roger's City around the time of Jack's funeral, allowing some to attend.

Matthew had remained home a while longer, but his job wouldn't wait forever. He had to go, catching ship at their next port.

"Have you got a new captain?" Her voice cracked on the last word. Jack's title.

"An older guy, well experienced, has hired on for this season at least before retiring. So, we'll see."

Annie nodded. Maybe Matthew would move into Jack's role in time. Jack had said he was ready.

Matthew flipped back the console between them and scooted over, gathering Annie into his arms. "I'm so sorry."

She held him tight. "Me, too."

He pulled back, his eyes watery and bright. "I let you down, Annie."

"No, you didn't." She shook her head and cupped his dear face. Matthew was her friend, too. What could he have possibly done to change what had happened to Jack? "It's only been a week, but I miss him."

Matthew kneaded her shoulders. "I know."

She welcomed the warmth of that rough massage. "Why did you leave right after the funeral?"

"I don't know." His voice softened. "I had to get away."

Annie chuckled. She'd felt the same way. She would have bolted if she could have gotten away with it. But the whole town had been there. Many of Jack's crew, too. And her mother-in-law would have tracked her down and dragged her back had she run.

"So, where've you been?" He hadn't stopped by but once to drop off Jack's things. She hadn't been home at the time. Returning from a walk, she'd missed him.

He let his hands drop from her shoulders and shrugged, not looking at her. "I was in the UP for a few days."

Annie nodded, wishing she could have escaped town for a while, too. A few times during the off-season, Jack had gone to the Upper Peninsula of Michigan to snowmobile with Matthew and his brothers. Jack had loved it. She patted Matthew's jeans-clad knee. "Well, be careful driving to catch ship."

He glanced at her hand and then studied her face. "I will."

She searched his serious expression. Something had changed in him. Annie could feel it. Something had changed in her, too. She pulled her hand back.

Matthew looked at her mouth.

Her heart pounded in her ears as he leaned closer and brushed his lips over hers. Featherlight and hesitant. He rested his forehead against hers and sighed. "Annie…"

Maybe he waited for encouragement or a sign to stop, but she could give neither. Matthew was warm and comforting. He understood her loss because he felt it, too.

Jack had left them both behind.

Matthew gripped her waist with big, strong hands. "I'm sorry."

"Me, too." They were repeating themselves.

A small voice warned her to back away, but she sought his lips once more. A comforting kiss between friends still grieving, that's all it was. A reminder that they hadn't died, too, even though it felt like they had.

But as the kiss grew deeper and more insistent, Annie fought against the sensation of drowning. Breathing hard, she pulled away. Her eyes burned like hot coals blistering with shame. How could she?

"I'm sorry," she choked out.

"Me, too." His voice wasn't steady, either.

Annie looked at the regret-filled horror on Matthew's face. She silently counted, but it was too late. She lost it.

Chapter One

April

"I can't be." Annie stared at the results with blurry eyes.

Fifteen years she'd been married to Jack. Ten of those years they'd tried to have a baby with no success. She'd switched to an organic diet, tried herbal remedies, fertility pills and shots that had made her sick, but nothing had worked.

Five years ago, she quit the ballet troupe in Grand Rapids and moved north with Jack to Maple Springs and set up shop as a dance instructor. Annie had gained a little weight since then but never enough. She'd never conceived. She'd accepted her fate and moved on.

But Jack had never stopped hoping.

Annie grabbed the box and reread the instructions. She'd followed them implicitly. How hard was it? She glanced at the test strip. The symbol was definitely showing a plus sign instead of a negative. And that plus sign grew darker.

Her stomach turned over. "Oh, Jack…"

Was this God's idea of a cruel joke? All these years they'd tried and failed. According to this test, they'd finally succeeded. But Jack would never see his own child. She closed her eyes, remembering the romantic Valentine's getaway they'd enjoyed at a ski resort near Traverse City. Neither of them skied, but Annie had been given a gift certificate from one of her clients for Christmas.

Was that when— If so, in a few months her belly would show and her in-laws would be heartsick when they found out. It'd be like losing Jack all over again if something went wrong.

Annie rubbed her temples. Jack's parents lived fifteen miles away in the town with the big grocery store. It's why she and Jack had chosen Maple Springs—close and yet far enough away. That and Jack had loved ice fishing and snowmobiling with Matthew during the off-season.

Annie had a hunch her in-laws were relieved they didn't need to deal with her now that their son was gone. Another twist of fate. Becoming grandparents would no doubt bring their paths back together. Marie was bound to be impossible. She'd never approved of anything Annie did. Annie was a *dancer*. It didn't matter that she'd been a professional ballerina, she might as well have come off the Vegas strip.

Tears spilled over and ran down her cheeks as she sat there, test still in hand. A knock at the front door made her jump.

"Annie?"

She stood at the sound of her friend, Ginger, coming inside. Annie blew her nose with a tissue and then threw the early pregnancy test into the powder-room trash can. Quickly, she washed her hands and left.

"I'm in the kitchen." Annie peeked out of the window into her backyard. Early daffodils had burst to life after what seemed like years in the deep freeze of a hard northern Michigan winter.

She leaned against the deep porcelain sink she'd found at an antique sale with Jack after they'd bought this house. They'd taken their time remodeling it room by room. Except for the roof. Jack was planning to do that this summer with Matthew's help.

Matthew...

The kiss they'd shared haunted her still. She might as well have a scarlet letter sewn across her heart reminding her how she'd betrayed Jack's memory. Matthew's embrace had been gentle when he awkwardly patted her back while she'd cried. The poor guy. Another poke to the heart from the needle that had stitched on that scarlet letter.

Her friend's high-heeled footsteps clicked on the tiled floor. "You okay? I know Easter Sunday at church is hard, but when I called this morning and got your answering machine, I got worried."

Annie sniffed. "I'm fine."

Her friend's eyes narrowed. "No, you're not. What's going on?"

She felt the tears stinging her eyes again. She'd been so emotional lately and thought it was all about grief, until she threw up and counted backward.

Ginger reached out her hands.

Annie took them, swallowing hard. She had to get a grip, but it felt as if she walked in a dream, like after she'd gotten word of Jack's death. In the weeks that had followed, she used to wander around in a daze. She'd often wake with a start, heart racing with fear before the pain came when reality hit that Jack was gone.

"I'm, ah…"

Ginger cocked her head. "Maybe you should sit down and tell me. You look a little flushed."

Annie slumped into a chair and ran her finger along

the grooves of her kitchen table. The burden didn't feel quite so heavy when it sunk in that she was finally going to have a baby. Something Jack had wanted for so long. A dream she'd given up on long ago.

Hope swelled and her spirits lifted, only to be dashed again. Jack wouldn't be there. He'd miss the birth of his own child.

Ginger touched her arm. "Annie?"

"I'm pregnant," she choked out. "A couple months, if I've counted right."

Ginger's eyes widened. They were big, anyway, but right now her friend's eyes reminded Annie of the brown speckled eggs she bought at the agricultural co-op a block over. "Oh, Annie, that's wonderful."

Annie ran her fingers through her hair, gripping it into a thick bundle at the nape of her neck. "Is it?"

"I'll make tea." Ginger went to the stove and grabbed the kettle. Once it was filled with water and settled over a high flame, she turned. "God's given you a gift."

A little late. She snorted. "Where was He five years ago with this gift?"

"Annie!" Ginger's voice dipped low. "Have you told anyone?"

Annie shook her head. "I just found out this morning with one of those store-bought tests. I'll wait until I see a doctor, to be sure."

But pregnancy confirmed what was happening to her body. It wasn't simply grief taking its toll. A new threat surfaced. One that scared her far more than raising a child alone. "I'm forty years old, Gin. What if I can't carry this baby to term?"

Ginger smiled. "You will. You can do this."

"I hope so." That was an understatement.

Annie grabbed ceramic mugs from the cupboard. The

teakettle's whistle blew, piercing the air. She filled her silver tea ball with loose leaves and tossed it in the pot. Then poured in hot water and let the tea steep all while the challenges of the future ahead flashed through her mind.

Annie slumped back in her chair. "I never considered raising a baby on my own. But I've got Jack's life insurance and the dance studio. I can bring a baby there, so I won't need to pay for day care for a while at least. It'll be fine. I'll be fine."

If Annie repeated that a few times, would she eventually believe it?

"Don't forget Jack's parents."

She gave her friend a sharp look. "I was trying to do just that."

Ginger laughed. She knew all about Annie's issues with her mother-in-law. "You know they'll help."

Annie looked at the pretty young woman who owned the shop where she bought her spices and loose tea and nodded. "That's what I'm worried about."

They went to the same church and had always been friendly, but Ginger had become a close friend after Jack died. After her aunt and sister returned to their homes in Arizona, Ginger had been the one holding out a safety ring when Annie thought she'd drown.

She still treaded water. Some days she'd slide under the waves and some days she'd float above them. With a baby on the way, she'd need to start floating way more than sinking. It's what Jack would expect of her. He'd want her to be happy.

May

Matthew Zelinsky walked along the downtown streets of his hometown where cottages lined the small harbor dug into the shoreline of northern Lake Michigan. The month of May meant that summer homes were finally opened up with cheery flowers dripping from their window boxes. The same went for gift shops clustered on Main Street. Even though he'd grown up here in Maple Springs, Michigan, the beauty of the area was never lost on him.

Some things never changed. Others changed too much. He missed Jack, his captain and friend. The new captain—Wyatt Williams was his name—was okay, but it wasn't the same. It'd never be the same again.

Matthew stepped out of the warm sunshine into the funky spice shop where Annie liked to buy her tea. The place was crowded. Summer residents had descended into the resort town a few days before Memorial Day weekend with its parade, craft fair and chicken BBQ.

Glancing at the line of big glass jars holding what looked like dried up weeds, he waited his turn. Was this the right thing to give a woman who regretted the kiss they'd shared?

Roses were out. Way too romantic. He was pretty sure Annie wanted none of that. She didn't eat real chocolate, either, and he refused to buy carob. He wouldn't know where to find the stuff. Chocolate implied romance, too, and he wasn't sure that's where he should go.

He had his regrets, as well. He wouldn't walk out on Annie as he'd done at the funeral. He didn't *need* to buy her anything but wanted Annie to know that this time, he'd be there if she needed him. Jack would want him to look out for her.

What would Jack think of him kissing his wife?

"Thou Shalt Not Covet Thy Neighbor's Wife..."

Matthew had learned his ten commandments as a kid and could recite them easily enough, but the last one took on new meaning. What kind of guy kissed a grieving widow a week after her husband's funeral?

The sounds of laughter erupted as more folks came inside. His turn had come and he stepped up to the counter.

The owner, Annie's friend, looked up. "Hi, Matthew. Welcome back."

"Hey, Ginger."

Jack and Annie had tried to fix him up with her, but Matthew hadn't been interested. No surprise there. Work on the Great Lakes took him away for months at a time. Most of the women he'd dated couldn't handle it. They'd call too often and complain too much when he didn't call back. There were dead zones out there, but that excuse had never flown very far. Drama. He hated all the drama.

Ginger smiled. "I heard your company hired on a new captain. How is he?"

Matthew rubbed the back of his neck. Was that all she'd heard? "He's okay. And temporary. For now."

"Good. What can I help you with?"

He perused the shelves loaded with names of spices and herbs he'd never heard of. "I'm looking for some tea."

She looked surprised. "For you?"

"For Annie." His cheeks burned. He forced himself to look Ginger in the eye. "You probably know what she likes. Give me whatever you think best."

Again, she smiled. Not an unkind smile, either. "I have just the thing."

He relaxed. A little. If Ginger knew anything about that kiss, she wasn't holding it against him. He wouldn't blame her if she did. He never should have let it go that far, but he'd sensed that Annie needed to be held. He'd needed to hold her, too. But after she'd kissed him back, something had snapped inside and let loose. So here he stood, buying apology tea.

Ginger removed the silver lid of a big glass container and scooped out the contents. The tea leaves looked like what he'd rake up from his parents' yard complete with little sticks.

"So, what are you up to for the next thirty days of free time?"

He shrugged. He needed to talk to Annie about her roof among other things. "I'm hoping to work on a building project, why?"

"No reason." She shrugged, too, as if she had something to say. Did she? "It's nice of you to buy tea for Annie. She'll enjoy this blend."

He cocked his head. "Yeah?"

"There's a little flyer in there with the ingredients and instructions." She handed him the brown paper bag stamped with *The Spice of Life* in dark green ink.

"Thanks. I'll be sure to tell her." He paid for his purchase and left.

Driving the three blocks from Ginger's store to Annie's Craftsman-style bungalow, he rehearsed the argument he'd give her for letting him replace the roof. The past two months had given him lots of time to think. And he'd thought about Annie Marshall practically every day of the sixty spent on his freighter.

He parked, got out and then stood on the walkway. Staring at her front porch, he gripped the paper bag Ginger had given him tighter. Good grief, this was Annie he was coming to see. He'd joked around with her for years, but Jack had always been there, too. Now he wasn't.

Annie was Jack's widow now.

He'd called her once in a while in port, but they hadn't said much. He couldn't broach the subject of that kiss. A phone call wasn't the best choice for that awkward conversation. It'd be better to talk to her in person. Like now.

He checked his watch. Ten-thirty was a respectable time to make a morning visit. He knew from what Jack had said that Annie's weekday dance lessons didn't start until after lunchtime. Had that changed?

He'd find out soon enough.

He gingerly ascended the wide front porch steps, remembering how he'd helped Jack and Annie move in after they'd bought the place. He'd also helped paint the exterior. She'd picked out the colors and called it *sage green*. She'd been adamant about pairing it with bright white trim. He and Jack had thought tan would look better.

He smiled, remembering how Annie had managed to get more paint on her than the house. He spotted her small car in the driveway and with a deep breath, knocked on the front door.

Nothing.

So he knocked again before he lost his nerve. Harder.

"Just a minute." Her voice sounded thin and far away, filtering through the screens of open windows.

It took a few moments before Annie finally opened the door. She wore socks that slouched around her ankles and shorts with a baggy T-shirt. Her thick, dark blond hair looked as though it had been pulled back in a hurry. She had a wet washcloth in her hand. Had she been cleaning?

"Maybe I should have called," Matthew said.

Her beautiful eyes widened with surprise. "That would have been a good idea."

He smiled, searched for some smart comment to tease her with and then frowned. She looked pale, and a sheen of sweat glistened on her forehead. "Hey, are you okay?"

Her face went white. She grasped the washcloth to her mouth and ran for the bathroom off the kitchen. He could hear her retch from where he stood, still on the porch.

Quietly, he entered and closed the door. "What's wrong, have you got the flu? I heard it's going around." Or was that old news he'd heard before going out on the lakes?

"Must be."

He could hear the water running as he made his way into the kitchen. He settled the bag of tea from Ginger's store on the counter and then filled the teakettle with fresh cold water, placed it on the stove and turned up the heat.

He'd never made tea from loose leaves before, but he'd watched Annie do it a thousand times. He fished around the utensil drawer until he found the silver ball he'd seen her use. Then he pulled out the plastic bag of tea and a piece of paper fluttered to the counter.

He glanced at the list of ingredients. *Ginger root, spearmint leaf, red raspberry leaf, orange peel, chamomile, peppermint leaf and lemon balm.*

What was lemon balm? Might as well be grass clippings.

He opened cupboards and then closed them.

"What are you doing?"

He turned, not liking the wary look in her eyes. "I'm looking for a teapot."

Her color hadn't returned. If anything, she looked even paler. And too thin. She'd lost weight. Annie's hair was wet, like she'd missed when splashing water on her face. She still managed to look beautiful, though. But fragile.

She came forward, her movements lithe and graceful. Annie had a dancer's body—long and lean even though she wasn't all that tall. He'd never gone to any of her performances. He wasn't a ballet kind of guy, but maybe he'd missed something special. She opened a lower cupboard, pulling out a round pink pot, and set it on the counter. Then she grabbed two mugs from an upper cupboard.

He leaned against the sink, out of her way. He would have kept the pot next to the cups considering they got used every day, but then he didn't have much in the way of dishes at his place so who was he to criticize.

She glanced at him. Wary.

"Thanks." Okay, yeah. Maybe he was a little afraid of her, too. Of touching her. Look what had happened the last time.

"Thank you for the tea." She peeked inside the bag and picked up the paper. Her eyes widened and her face flushed.

He reached out and touched her shoulder. Felt her tremble. "You sure you're okay?"

"Fine. Yes. I'll be fine."

She didn't look fine. She looked upset, like she might even cry. He prayed she wouldn't cry. That night her sobs had torn him in two.

Annie had lost her husband. The husband they both loved. He'd turn back the clock if he could. Matthew wished a thousand times over that he'd taken Jack's comment about heartburn after dinner more seriously. If only he'd known. But then they'd eaten hot wings for dinner and nearly everyone on board had heartburn.

Still, he couldn't shake the feeling that he'd let Annie down by not keeping Jack safe. Keeping everyone safe on ship was part of his job. His responsibility. He couldn't help but feel as if he'd failed when it came to Jack.

The teakettle whistle blew through the silence, shattering his thoughts.

Annie bustled forward and turned off the gas.

Matthew touched her arm again. Why'd he keep touching her? "I've got this. Sit down before you fall down."

She looked at him with a raised chin. Annie didn't like him telling her what to do. Her soft blue eyes had yellow rings around the pupils. Pretty eyes made even prettier framed with thick, dark lashes. She nodded, crumpled up the paper that came with the tea and sat down.

He felt her watchful eyes burning holes into his back as he stuffed the clippings in the silver ball and tossed it into the pot. No doubt she'd jump in if he did it wrong.

Next, he dumped in hot water and settled the lid in place and then set it on the table in front of her. He slid into the opposite chair and handed Annie a mug.

"You want any?"

"Ah, no." He was a strong coffee kind of guy and he'd already had his fill this morning. Still, he watched her pour herself a cup of the rust-colored water.

She sniffed it, took a tentative sip and then a deep breath. Waited and then another sip.

"Does it help?"

Her eyes flew open wide. "Help what?"

"Your stomach. You just threw up, remember?"

Her cheeks flushed a pretty shade of pink. "Yeah."

He smiled, at an odd loss for words. He'd never had to try hard to talk to her before. He grabbed the paper ball she'd crumpled and smoothed it back out. The name on the other side smacked hard.

Morning Sickness Tea.

He handed it back to her. "What does this mean?"

Annie looked up like a scared rabbit, ready to dart for cover. "Look, Matthew—"

"Are you going to have a baby?"

Her eyes filled with tears, and she shrugged.

"Don't you know for sure?" His voice sounded much too shrill.

Annie looked fierce. "Yes, I'm sure."

Matthew sat back, stunned. "Wow."

"Yeah, wow. Please don't tell anyone about the baby."

His gaze narrowed. "Why?"

Her eyes clouded over. "Please?"

He knew how badly Jack had wanted kids. He'd put on a good front with his wife and often acted as if it didn't matter. But Matthew knew how deep Jack's disappointment ran. And now, the guy would never see his own kid.

He sighed. "I won't say anything."

"Thank you."

"But I'll help."

Annie's eyes narrowed. "What are you talking about?

Matthew stood up and paced the kitchen. He'd blurted out that offer without thinking, but it felt right. "Starting with the roof—"

"Matthew, please. Don't do this because you feel guilty over a silly kiss. We were both vulnerable that night."

Irritation ripped through him. Hearing her words made him feel cheap. And there was nothing silly about that kiss. Cliché, maybe, but it had shaken his world pretty good. "Will you let me finish?"

She fluttered her fingers. "Fine, go ahead."

"Are those shingles for the roof still in the garage?"

She looked confused. "I don't know. I guess."

"I'd like to take care of the roof while I'm off for the next few weeks."

"No." She shook her head. "Don't worry about it. I can call someone."

Of course she was going to be difficult. "I want to do it."

She stood, too, and went to the sink. "Just let it go."

Matthew wanted to, but couldn't *just let it go.* "Annie…"

She faced him. "I mean it. I'm not your responsibility. I can take care of myself."

"I never said you couldn't. I promised Jack I'd help him with the roof and I want to honor that promise."

She stared him down.

He stared back.

This was about his promise to Jack. Not her. It couldn't be about her. But deep inside, he knew it was all about her. He couldn't help it. He cared. He'd always cared. And now, with a baby on the way, she'd need someone to lean on. That someone might as well be him.

"I need to do it. Don't you get that?"

Her eyes softened. "I just—" She went pale again and pursed her lips. Her forehead broke out into a sweat.

He went to her. "Come on—you should probably lie down. We can talk about this later."

"I'm fine."

Obviously, she wasn't. Stubborn woman. "I'll carry you if I have to."

She gave him one challenging look and then grabbed her mug and headed for the living room. She moved pretty fast for someone who needed morning sickness tea.

Round one with Annie.

He smiled as he followed her.

At least he'd won.

Annie sank onto the couch. She wasn't about to lie down in front of Matthew, so she pulled her feet up under her and leaned against the arm. She took another sip of tea and waited for the nausea to pass. It always passed.

"Do you want me to get your pillow?" Matthew asked.

"No." She wanted to wipe that caring look off his handsome face. And stop the jitters in her stomach when he looked at her like that.

His skin was already tanned from the sun. Lines cut across his forehead and around his eyes, but not from age. His skin looked weathered from being out on deck where the spring winds chafed. Rugged.

But he was still young, thirty-one, maybe thirty-two by now. He grabbed the afghan from the chair by the fireplace and draped it over her with strong hands that could be so gentle.

"Thanks." Any minute now, she'd tell him to leave.

Why was he being so nice? But then, Matthew had always been nice. Jack had once told her how Matthew had nursed an injured seagull back to health. A seagull! Jack had called them rats with wings. She had a lot more than a broken wing. She didn't want to take advantage of that kindness.

"Just take it easy." He tucked the blanket's edge behind her shoulder, coming much too close for comfort.

She glanced up and the sharp retort poised on her tongue died the moment she spied confusion wash across his face.

His eyes darted to her mouth.

She held her breath, powerless. The air hummed with this new awareness of each other. This awkward attraction snatched their words and they ended up staring. Remembering, maybe even reliving, that kiss they'd shared.

He abruptly stood and backed away. "I'm going to check the garage for those shingles and then go. Call me if you need anything, okay?"

"Okay." She wasn't going to call.

At the door he paused. "Annie?"

"Yeah?"

"I'm going to help with the baby. Jack would want me to."

"Matthew—"

But he'd already closed the door.

Annie let loose a sigh. A nugget of hope blossomed

and grew. Matthew was right. Jack would want him to help her out because it would help Matthew heal, too. He was the brother Jack never had and probably the only man Jack trusted implicitly.

But Annie didn't want to depend on Matthew. He couldn't fill the void that Jack left behind, and needing someone hurt all the more when they were gone.

Chapter Two

The next day, Annie was in the kitchen when she heard the quick knock on her front door. She gulped the rest of her tea and headed for the living room. She was grateful for Ginger's choice. The calming blend eased her morning sickness, but she wished that Matthew hadn't found out. She didn't want anyone to know about the baby until it was safe. Not until she reached that halfway mark. Not until she'd received a good report from the ultrasound.

Another rat-a-tat, and then the door opened. "Annie?" *Matthew.*

"Morning." She smiled. She'd decided to support his repair-the-roof effort. It'd help him repay what he thought he owed Jack.

Matthew didn't smile in return. He looked stormy despite the bright sunshine outside. "Don't you keep your door locked?"

She blinked at his sharp tone. Who'd he think he was talking to her like that? This was Maple Springs, not her town house in Grand Rapids. "Sometimes. And if you must know, I was already up and out this morning."

She'd gone to her doctor for her second appointment.

She'd been labeled *high-risk* due to her age and history of fertility problems. Not welcome news.

Matthew stepped into the living room, followed by a younger version of him. "This is my brother Luke. We're going to take a look at the roof."

"Nice to meet you, Luke." Annie stepped forward and offered the young man her hand. He was also tall, broad-shouldered and had light brown hair and bright blue eyes.

"You, too." When he smiled, he resembled Matthew even more.

"Luke's a roofer with our uncle over the summer months when he's not in college. With his help, we'll crank this out in no time."

She didn't like the idea of either one spending their downtime working on her house. "Let me know how much a job like this costs, so I can pay you the going rate."

"Nope. It's just the materials," Matthew answered before his brother had a chance. "I'll give you a list."

She planted her hands on her hips. "Wait just a minute. You can't expect your brother to work for free."

Matthew grinned. "He's not. We've got our own deal."

Annie glanced at Luke.

"I'm going to move in with him. Matty and Cam are putting me up for the summer at no rent." Luke winked at her. "Your roof's not that big so this should be a snap."

That was no deal. That sounded more like slave labor. Annie started to argue. "Now, look here—"

"Luke, there's a ladder in the garage," Matthew cut her off. He hadn't looked away from her, either. "Why don't you check out the existing shingles? I'll be out in a minute."

Heat infused her body as she stared him down. Any minute now steam was bound to blow from her nostrils. This was still her house! Since when had Matthew turned tyrant?

"Sure." Luke looked between them and then left.

"You can't just take over." Annie's voice came out shrill.

"I'm helping you." His eyes blazed with something fierce and protective.

She snorted. "Are you? Are you really?"

"I'm trying to!" He stepped closer and sighed. "Look, I'm sorry. But Luke doing this is nothing you need be concerned about. He's itching to get out of Mom and Dad's, and Cam and I are gone most of the summer."

She didn't like it, but nodded. If Matthew's little brother welcomed the arrangement, who was she to champion him? Matthew had refused payment from Jack, as well, when they'd talked about doing the roof. It's what friends did for each other, right?

She remembered the conversation between the two men over pizza. They'd been going through pictures of their scuba-diving trip to the Manitou Islands on a rare week of scheduled time off together. They'd gone through the Manitou passage hundreds of times with the freighter but had wanted to dive the area. Scattered in those northern Lake Michigan waters lay dozens of past shipwrecks that Annie would rather not think about let alone see.

She swallowed a wave of upset. Her nausea came and went. She usually felt fine by afternoon into evening. The doctor had said that her morning sickness was a good sign, but she'd still require close monitoring throughout her pregnancy. She didn't want to lose this baby after years of trying and failing.

"What is it?" He touched her elbow.

Annie came back to the present. "What?"

"You were far away just now. You okay?"

"Fine."

He gave her a long look but didn't push. "We'll be up on the roof figuring out what we need. It won't take long."

"I'd like a copy of that list, you know, so I can pay for the materials." Annie turned to go. "Oh, and Matthew?"

He leaned against the front door. His presence filled the room. He was only a few inches taller than Jack, yet today Matthew seemed so much larger than her late husband. "Yeah?"

This was harder to say than she'd expected. She didn't like people doing her favors, but having someone she could trust take care of her roof was comforting all the same. "Thank you."

"You're welcome. Do me a favor?"

"Yeah?"

"Keep your door locked." He gave her a nod and left.

Annie stared at the door and wrestled with that request, knowing he'd made it with good intentions. Matthew was home for only a month before heading back out on the lakes for two or three. By the time he returned home again, she'd be huge. Would she make it that far?

"Please God…" Annie whispered, and then paused.

She hadn't prayed much lately. In fact, she'd stopped talking to God after Jack's death. Oh, she'd cried a lot, and even shouted her anger and confusion for losing her husband without notice.

Why'd God take Jack when he'd never been diagnosed with heart disease? As far as she knew, it didn't even run in his family. How were they supposed to prevent something they had no knowledge of? How was that fair? Wasn't God supposed to play fair?

But God was God. And God had taken Jack.

Annie's eyes burned. She was finally going to have

a baby. A sweet treasure Jack had wanted for so long. A gift she'd still never be able to give him.

What if God took her baby, too?

Resting her hands on the slightest swell of her middle, Annie didn't want to think about how she'd abused her body for years to dance. Staying reed-thin for lead parts and lift partners. Punishment, her mother-in-law called it. She'd punished her body for years and that's why she couldn't conceive.

Annie's whisper came out on a ragged breath. "Please Lord, keep this baby safe."

The next morning, Matthew walked into the warm kitchen of his parents' home. His mom stirred something on the stove that smelled like maple so he snuck close and peeked over her shoulder. "What's for breakfast? Pancakes?"

"Matthew!" Helen Zelinsky clutched the base of her neck and laughed. "I didn't hear you come in."

He spied the saucepan of steaming oatmeal and grimaced. He'd grown up on the stuff and never once ate it since moving out. "Got any bacon?"

"Maybe. Now get out of my way. There's fresh coffee in the pot."

Matthew didn't hesitate to fix a cup. Then he pulled out a chair and sat down. The kitchen table had been set with bowls, small glasses for juice, milk and a bottle of maple syrup made in the Zelinsky sugar shack. He knew the routine. A hot breakfast was a must according to his mom no matter what the season.

"Matthew." His father nodded as he entered the kitchen. "What brings you here this early?"

A tall man who'd retired from a long career in the Army, Andy Zelinsky had started a maple syrup operation years ago. Matthew's parents spent their golden summers into fall manning booths at craft fairs all over northern Michigan to sell their product. They didn't do too badly, either.

"I'm picking up Luke. We're going to work on Annie Marshall's roof this week." They'd purchased the supplies they needed and were ready to start. He bent down and petted the cat. Tigger butted his head against Matthew's ankles, purring like mad.

His father poured juice in a glass. "Nice of you to help out there."

His parents had gone to Jack's funeral. They knew the situation. Jack had been to their house with him on many occasions to ice-fish since his folks had inland lake frontage. And Jack had bought Zelinsky syrup every Christmas for Annie.

Midsip of his coffee, he paused and set the cup back down. He'd have to make sure Annie got her half gallon this year. When would the baby be born? Surely, by Christmas.

He grabbed a bowl and spoon. "I was going to help Jack with it this summer, anyway."

"How is Annie? Poor woman." His mom set the pan of oatmeal on a pad and then retreated for a plate of bacon from the microwave.

Matthew grabbed a couple slices before she set it down.

His mom slapped his hand. "We need to pray first."

He popped the bacon in his mouth and gasped. "Hot."

His mother chuckled. "See, *Bozia* punish."

Matthew shook his head. Those were his grandmother's words. He'd heard them all his life, but this time they stopped him cold. Did God really punish? If so, what might be in store for him for breaking the tenth commandment?

"So answer my question." His mom gave him a sharp look.

"What question?" He reached for another piece of bacon and set it on his napkin.

"How is Annie Marshall?"

He shrugged. "She's holding her own."

How's a woman supposed to be when her husband recently died? Add a baby on the way and it was a wonder Annie still got out of bed, let alone yammer at him for bringing his brother to work on the roof.

The image of Annie with her hands on her hips flashed through his mind. She was even prettier riled up. Why'd he always notice how she looked?

"So sad." His mother slipped into a chair and served up oatmeal into bowls.

"Yeah."

"Hey." His youngest brother entered the kitchen dressed in old jeans and a T-shirt. At twenty years old, Luke still lived at home when he wasn't away at college.

"Now, we can bless the food." His father bowed his head.

They all recited the simple prayer his family had used forever. "Bless us, O Lord! and these Thy gifts, which we are about to receive from Thy bounty, through Christ our Lord. Amen."

"Amen." Matthew poured syrup over his oatmeal, crumpled bacon on top and dug in.

"Uncle John said we've got three weeks before his contractor's account needs to be paid." Luke stuffed bacon into his mouth.

Matthew nodded. "No problem."

"You're not paying for her roof—" His mom started.

"Leave him be, Helen."

Matthew nodded toward his father. "She's paying for the materials. Luke asked Uncle John if we could use his account for the discount."

"Let's hurry up and get over there." Luke didn't linger, nor did he believe in wasting time. But then, he winked. "I want to see you two argue again."

"Argue?" His mom asked, horrified.

"You should have seen them stare each other down like a couple of alley cats." Luke grinned.

"Matthew! Why were you arguing with her?"

He kicked his brother under the table, connecting with Luke's boot instead of anything that might hurt.

His kid brother's grin only got wider.

"Annie doesn't accept my help very well," Matthew finally replied.

His father's eyebrows rose.

His mom exchanged a look with his dad before she said, "Honey, be careful. She's still grieving and probably vulnerable."

"Sure, Mom."

Too late. He'd already kissed her. He wouldn't admit *that* to his mother. Bad enough, he wanted to do it again. That tenth commandment came to mind. Was it considered coveting when the neighbor's wife was now a widow?

Matthew polished off the rest of his oatmeal and another slice of bacon and then looked at Luke. "Ready?"

"I was born ready."

Matthew chuckled. "Let's go."

It was a short drive to Annie's. The Zelinsky farm lay only ten miles north of town on fifty acres wedged between a small inland lake and state land. By the time they arrived, the truck hauling a rented Dumpster had already backed far into Annie's driveway. She'd left her car parked out front as he'd asked when he'd called her last night. She'd sounded tired, sad even, but told him she was fine. She was always fine. He'd heard that statement too many times to believe it.

After inspecting the roof yesterday, Luke had suggested they tear off the old shingles that were too worn for an overlay. Matthew had agreed even though it pulled his brother away from his summer job a couple more days. Good thing the kid worked for a relative who happened to own the largest roofing company in the area. They'd pulled a permit and rented a Dumpster lickety-split.

Matthew didn't want to cut corners and he didn't want leaks cropping up because he hadn't been thorough. Like that night Jack had complained after eating those hot wings. Matthew should have offered his friend aspirin instead of antacids. That small move might have saved Jack's life.

In the backyard, Luke steadied the ladder. He had a couple of garden forks in hand, ready to climb up onto the roof. "Once we've stripped off the old shingles, we'll know for sure the condition underneath."

Matthew looked through the kitchen window, expecting to see Annie there at the sink. Odd. She hadn't come out. She knew they were coming this morning. The beeping of the Dumpster delivery would have cued her in to that fact. Was she okay? Or maybe still sick.

"I'll be up in a minute."

Luke grinned. "Take your time."

Matthew ignored the knowing expression on his brother's face and tried the back door. It opened easily. Unlocked. But then it was nine in the morning and

Annie had probably left the door open after she'd moved her car before they arrived. No need to get riled up. Yet.

He poked his head into the laundry room. "Annie?"

No answer.

He stepped into the small kitchen. It smelled like cinnamon. She put that spice in a lot of the dishes she made including her tea. Jack used to complain about Annie nagging him to eat weird stuff like sprouts and tofu sausage. She was something of a health-food nut and nearly vegetarian to boot. She ate fish, though. Annie loved grilled fish whenever he and Jack brought home a load of perch caught ice fishing during the shipping off-season.

"Annie?"

"Hmm?" Her muffled voice sounded from the living room.

"You feeling okay?" He walked softly toward her.

She was curled up on the sofa, sleeping under a knitted afghan. Her thick hair lay in a mass of dark blond waves on the throw pillow. It glimmered like gold, caught in a beam of sunlight streaming through the windows.

He slammed his hands in his pockets to keep from threading his fingers through all that hair.

Surely, she hadn't slept there all night. Then he noticed the laptop on the floor, lid up but screen dark. And a mess of invoices lay stacked next to it. He recognized the double-M logo of her dance studio, Marshall Movement. She must have been working and had fallen asleep—but it was now nine in the morning. Was she not sleeping well at night?

Quietly, he returned to the backyard. Up the ladder, he joined his brother on the roof.

"Everything okay?" Luke handed him one of the garden forks.

"I don't know." Matthew slipped on his work gloves

and started tearing off old shingles. They tossed them in the rented Dumpster as they went. "She's sleeping."

Luke's eyes widened. "You went upstairs?"

"She was on the couch." Matthew tried to shrug off his concern, but it stayed close and pestered.

Annie could take care of herself. He knew that. But was she? He'd never known her to look so pale and weak. Was that due to morning sickness, or was grief dragging her down, too? Matthew aimed to find out and help where he could.

"Lunch is here," Annie yelled up the ladder, squinting in the bright sunshine.

Matthew's head popped into view. "Lunch?"

"Pizza. I had it delivered." Annie felt pretty good considering her morning was officially shot. She had woken up at seven, fallen back asleep and now it was noon. Her first dance class wasn't until two this afternoon, so she had time to get a few things done before she left.

The guys climbed down the ladder, washed up at the laundry room sink, then joined her on the back deck.

"Thanks." Luke popped the lid of the pizza box and dug in.

Matthew poured a cup of pop from the two-liter.

"There's water in the cooler, too. Help yourself. It's supposed to be hot today." Annie grabbed a water bottle and sat down under the market umbrella that shaded her deck table and chair set. She had to eat something, so a handful of crackers and some plain Greek yogurt would have to do. She hoped.

"Aren't you going to join us?" Matthew pulled two slices of steaming pepperoni-and-cheese onto a paper plate and sat next to her.

She wrinkled her nose at the smell of grease. "Not sure I can do pizza even picking off the meat."

He gave her meager lunch a long look. "Did you eat this morning?"

Annie wouldn't meet his eyes. "I had a little something."

"What?"

Her eyes flashed. "Toast, okay?"

"Dude—" Luke started, but Matthew silenced him with a hard look.

Annie was glad Matthew didn't defend his overbearing concern, but she gave his brother her sympathy. "He thinks he's helping."

Luke laughed and bit into the steaming pizza.

While the men ate, Annie looked over her backyard. She usually put in a small garden in the corner. Memorial weekend had always been her planting time, but she hadn't so much as tilled the soil yet. Too tired. When would she stop feeling so tired?

And alone.

She was used to Jack gone for months at a time out on the lakes, but knowing he'd never come back had set her adrift.

She spotted strips of torn shingles hanging from the Dumpster and littering the ground where the guys had missed. Too easily, she could picture her husband making jokes about their aim and her heart twisted.

"Thank you for lunch." Matthew's serious-sounding voice caught her attention.

She looked at him. His nose was sunburned. The yellow T-shirt he wore was damp and dirty in spots, but he smelled good, like fresh air and sunshine. She even sniffed a hint of spice when he moved.

Matthew was definitely a handsome man but she had

no business noticing. So why'd she feel this pull toward him? Was it their shared grief or her crazy hormones kicking in? How could she find him attractive so soon after the husband she loved had died?

He looked at her, too, his gaze locked with hers.

He was never far from her thoughts these days. Could Matthew read them, too? She cleared her throat. "It's the least I can do considering the work you guys are doing. How does it look up there?"

"Good," Luke mumbled around a mouthful. "No damage underneath the old shingles."

"I'll leave the back door unlocked when I leave. There's a bathroom off the kitchen. Help yourself to anything in the fridge, too." She nibbled a cracker.

Luke stood with another piece of pizza in hand. "Thanks, Annie." He grabbed a bottle of water from the cooler and nodded toward his brother. "I'm going back up."

"I'll be a sec."

Luke nodded and left.

Annie stood, as well, uncomfortable sitting alone with Matthew. "I'll get you my credit card."

He touched her arm. "No need. I'll have an invoice prepared with a detailed list of items purchased from the hardware store. We used our uncle's account so you've got three weeks to pay on it."

"Oh." She slumped back into her chair, feeling a little nauseous and lost, but oddly comforted by his touch.

She looked at him.

He looked back.

Really, what could they talk about? They'd never had trouble with conversation before, but it was different now. They were different. She tipped her head back against her chair and closed her eyes, willing the upset in her belly to settle.

Matthew's fingertips slid to her hand. "You okay?"

That gentle gesture zinged up her arm. "Fine. I just— Can you close that pizza box?"

Her skin cooled where his fingers had been as he secured the cardboard lid and pushed the offensive pizza away.

Annie finally opened her eyes. "I should get ready for my class."

"Maybe you should skip today." He sounded worried.

"Oh, no." She popped out of her seat. "I'm fine. Really."

Matthew didn't look as if he believed her. In fact, he looked irritated.

Welcome to the club.

Irritation and worry were Annie's daily companions, lined up behind the empty feeling of loss. Right now she couldn't take the concern in Matthew's eyes. Nor the desire to lean on him. He had broad shoulders that she'd cried against before. She didn't want to do it again or she might not stop.

"So what did the doctor say about all this?"

"The usual stuff, I suppose." Annie didn't want to admit her fears or that high-risk label. It'd only make Matthew worry that much more. She didn't want him hovering too close, either.

"When will it be born?" Matthew pressed.

"It?" She laughed when his cheeks reddened.

"He, she… I don't know what to say."

Annie patted his shoulder and felt his muscles tense beneath her touch. "Before Thanksgiving."

"That's before the close of the shipping season." Matthew stood up and faced her.

Why'd he look so concerned? "Yeah, so?"

"So…I want to be there."

Annie's stomach flipped but she shook her head. What was he thinking offering up something like that? "I'll be fine. Ginger can go with me."

The curse of every single mother reduced to having their friends there for delivery instead of the baby's father. She and Jack would have had all winter together with their child. And now?

Christmas was going to be horrible this year.

Matthew saw too much and stood too close. "Aww, Annie."

Annie backed away before she did something stupid like pulling him into her arms. Those broad shoulders of his were calling out for another good cry.

One, two, three…

Her tongue felt dry and thick, but she managed to say, "I'll see you tomorrow."

The following evening, Matthew stepped inside Annie's dance studio. She'd taken over a space once used as an exercise gym. The storefront remained a wall of windows that Annie had covered with see-through fabric framed by maroon velvet curtains. The other walls were covered with mirrors. Classical music played softly over the sound system.

A few people that he assumed might be parents lingered while Annie worked with a group of young girls. They stood in a single line and gripped a waist-high bar.

"First, second, third…" Annie called out the numbers as she moved into different positions. Up on her toes, down, pointed leg out, back in.

Her students followed her lead.

Annie didn't use a bar and she moved with fluid grace.

Her hair had been twined into a knot at the back of her head making her neck look long like the rest of her. She wore a leotard over black leggings and a filmy skirt. Her stomach looked as trim as the rest of her.

Jack had met Annie at a coffee shop in Grand Rapids where she'd been a ballerina with a company there. She'd left performing behind when they moved north and set up this studio. If he remembered correctly, she taught both ballet and exercise—advanced stretching or something.

Annie caught him watching her and faltered.

He smiled. She must have been beautiful on stage.

Checking her watch, Annie announced. "Okay, ladies, that's it for today. Nice job."

A chorus of "aww" rang out.

While she talked to parents, he toured the wall of fame decorated with pictures of local dance productions Annie had been involved with and previous students that had gone beyond what this area had to offer.

He turned when he heard her approach.

"Sorry." Her face flushed. No, her skin glowed. But that could be from the sheen of healthy perspiration along her forehead. She wiped it away with a towel and then looked up at him. "What are you doing here?"

Good question. "I thought I'd go over the invoice that lists out the roofing materials with you."

She tipped her head. "You could have brought it over tomorrow."

"I was on my way home and thought maybe you'd want to grab dinner." Showing Annie what she paid for on the roof was reason enough to stop by. But then, maybe it was about spending time with her, too, making sure she was okay. Stopping by her house later wasn't a good idea, and tomorrow, he'd be busy with the roof, hurried along by Luke.

"Dinner, huh?" She looked wary.

"Are you feeling up to it?"

Then annoyed. "You don't have to worry about me, you know."

"I know." So why was he? He thought about her a lot. Maybe too much. "But we both have to eat."

She smiled. "I am hungry and cooking doesn't sound appealing tonight."

"I'll even let you pick the place." He smiled back.

That earned him an evil look of mischief like the old Annie. "There's a new restaurant down the street that's good."

Matthew got nervous considering what Annie thought was good food. "Do they serve real meat?"

"Yes." She chuckled and sat down to unlace the ribbons of her ivory-colored ballet shoes with the square toes.

"Does it hurt?"

"Does what hurt?" She pulled off a sheer footie sock.

"Standing on your toes like that."

Annie stretched out bare feet and wiggled her skinny, calloused toes that were taped in places. "I've exercised them all my life to make them strong, so I'm used to it. But my feet are ugly."

He'd never noticed her feet before. They looked work-hardened but not bad. "I've seen prettier."

She clobbered him in the shoulder but laughed. It sounded good hearing her laugh. "Let me throw on a cover-up and we'll go."

"I'll be right here." He meant it, too. She could lean on him. "Always here for you. I hope you know that."

She nodded. After scooping up her ballet shoes, she entered her windowed office and slipped on a baggy cotton dress over her dance clothes. Annie turned off the lights and swung a big purse over her shoulder before coming back to stand before him. She'd slipped into cloth-like flats that barely covered her feet.

"After you." She opened the door for him.

He stepped outside and waited while she locked up. "How far is it?"

Annie shrugged. "About a block away. Do you mind walking?"

"Not at all." He almost reached for her hand.

This felt a lot like a date. Was he trying to date Annie Marshall? Surely, it was too soon to go there.

He glanced at the woman walking beside him. She was a few years older than him. Not that it mattered. Not to him. The fine lines near her eyes didn't detract a bit. She'd always been beautiful. And ageless, like one of those models he'd see on infomercials sharing their fountain-of-youth secrets.

Annie caught him staring. "What?"

"Nothing." He really needed to cover this awkward awareness or they'd have an uncomfortable dinner together. "I was just picturing your feet."

She rolled her eyes. "Real nice."

It felt good to tease her. Like they were friends again and nothing had happened to change that. There was no reason to let one kiss change what they were. They were friends. He needed to remember that.

Chapter Three

"Thanks for dinner." Annie snuggled deeper against the passenger seat of Matthew's truck. She should have stood her ground and walked home like normal. It might have energized her after dinner. The restaurant was only a few blocks from her house, but Matthew wouldn't hear of it.

Matthew turned onto her street. "No problem."

After the cold, damp month of April, May had whispered in with warm days, but the evenings still turned cool.

It was still daylight at nine in the evening as the sun hadn't quite set. One of the many advantages of living in northern Michigan was the long days summer provided.

She let loose a yawn and her eyelids drooped.

"Tired?"

"Yeah. I ate way too much."

Matthew chuckled. "I'm glad you've got your appetite back."

Tonight, her appetite had returned with a vengeance. She'd eaten everything in sight while Matthew went over the list of materials purchased for her roof. She'd told him not to worry, that she trusted him, but he'd been thorough, anyway. He wanted her to know what he and his brother were doing and why.

He pulled into her driveway and put the truck in park then turned toward her. "I'm worried about you."

Annie stared straight ahead. "Don't be. Please? I'm working through this."

"You don't have to do it alone. I'm right here."

Annie looked at Matthew's earnest face. It'd be easy to depend on him. And too easy to repeat the kiss that had happened in this same truck. She wasn't going to do that to him. It wasn't fair to trap him into something that was merely grief-driven, or worse. Maybe this was about hormones.

She forced a smile. "I know you are, and I appreciate it. You don't owe me anything, Matthew."

He looked relieved, but troubled. "I know."

She cupped his cheek and smiled. "I'm okay."

He leaned toward her, only slightly, and then stopped. His blue eyes searched hers.

Annie pulled her hand back before her overactive hormones kicked her into trouble. Again. "Good night, Matthew."

"Good night."

She slipped out of his truck. Bounding up the stairs onto the porch, she turned and waved before unlocking her door. He didn't leave. She knew he wouldn't leave until she was safely inside.

And behind a locked door.

In the dining room, she peeked through the curtains. Matthew waved then left. He treated her like glass since he'd come home. Maybe because she'd shattered so quickly after that kiss.

Her purse vibrated, so she pulled out her cell phone. "Hello?"

"Annie, where are you? I was getting worried." Ginger had called twice according to her missed calls.

"Sorry, I went out to dinner and forgot to switch my phone back to a ringtone after dance class. What's up?"

"I wanted to see how you're feeling."

Annie clamped down irritation. Really, she should be thankful that she had good friends. People who cared. But she wasn't twelve years old and staying home alone for the first time. "I'm fine."

"Wait, who'd you go to dinner with?"

"I went with Matthew."

"Oh?"

Annie knew that tone well. She wasn't biting on her friend's tell-me-more interest. "What's with that stunt in selling him morning sickness tea?"

"He asked what you'd like, so that seemed like the perfect choice because you needed something for the nausea." She sounded innocent enough. "Does it help?"

"Yes, but I didn't want anyone to know. Not yet." Annie plopped onto the couch and kicked off her shoes before putting her feet up.

Despite the red nail polish on her toes, she'd always have ugly feet. How many times had her mother-in-law said it was unnatural to go *en pointe*?

"So, he figured it out?"

"Yeah, and now he's redoing my roof." Annie wiggled her toes.

"Out of the blue, he's replacing your roof?"

"No. He and Jack were going to do it this summer, during their shared week off. Matthew wanted to keep that promise. His brother is helping him."

"Uh-huh."

Was that sarcasm she heard? "Ginger—"

"Sounds to me like he's doing this for you because he cares."

"Of course he cares. He was Jack's best friend." Annie's stomach tipped and rolled.

Gas bubbles? And small wonder after the meal she'd eaten. This weird feeling had more to do with her digestion than any dawning attraction to Matthew. She'd read about what to expect in the months ahead. She shouldn't feel the baby's movements for a least another couple weeks to a month.

"That's not what I meant."

Annie knew exactly what Ginger meant. "It's way too soon."

Her friend snorted. "Says who?"

"Seriously? Anyone would think it's too soon. Besides, how can I even think about someone else after Jack?"

"Jack's gone, hon." Ginger's voice grew soft and full of sympathy. "It's okay to care for someone new. Especially someone who understands what you're going through. Matthew knows how much this hurts."

Annie's throat grew tight. That's what was scary. Matthew knew her well. He felt what she felt. But half of her also felt dead. Grief had a way of numbing emotions, and some feelings never came back. Not exactly a prize for a guy as sweet as Matthew Zelinsky. He deserved better. He deserved someone whole. And someone young.

The next day, Matthew took in his and Luke's handiwork from atop Annie's home. The roof was nearly done. With rain forecasted for the looming Memorial Day weekend, they'd finish up in the nick of time. He stretched and yawned.

He spotted Annie resting in a lounge chair after she'd

spent the morning weeding her flower beds. Her small garden plot lay untouched and unready for planting. Now that it was only her, maybe she didn't want to plant vegetables.

That small reminder of Jack's death hit him like a punch in the gut as a sense of loss swamped him. Jack had always bragged about his wife's cucumbers and tomatoes and onions. He used to bring bags of her homegrown veggies onto the laker. Matthew hated the thought of Annie giving it up.

She hadn't moved from that lounge chair in a while. Had she fallen asleep again? Dressed in loose overall shorts and a T-shirt, Annie had a large floppy hat covering her face so he couldn't tell if she was awake or not.

He checked his watch. Nearly noon. "Hey, I'm going to buzz home real quick."

"What for?" Luke took a long swig from his water bottle.

The sun scorched them both and lunch would be a welcome break.

"I'm going to grab that fish we caught last night. We can grill it here for lunch." Maybe that'd bolster Annie's spirits. She loved a fresh catch.

"Good idea."

Matthew climbed down the ladder. "Anything you want to go with it?"

"Coleslaw."

He nodded. Annie had been feeding him and his little brother every day. Lunch was ordered in or picked up from the corner IGA store. They'd had pizza, sub sandwiches and even a bucket of fried chicken. Stuff Annie didn't eat. Today, he'd grill something for her and maybe pick up a couple funky salads, too. Annie liked a lot of greens. She'd eaten a whole plateful of rabbit food last night at dinner.

It didn't take long to buy what he needed. The small house he shared with one of his older brothers—and soon Luke—sat on the edge of town. Right near the locally owned and operated grocery store. In less than half an hour, he was back at Annie's lighting the gas grill.

Luke worked on the roof while he grilled and Annie continued to snooze. The woman could really sleep. Did the baby sap her energy, or was it depression? Grief could fall into despair.

He prayed Annie wasn't so wrecked by Jack's death that she couldn't sleep at night. She had smiled, though. Laughed even. With him. So he had hope that she was making her way back.

He stepped inside to gather plates, utensils and glasses full of ice. Annie kept the cooler outside stocked with water and pop. She'd also made sun tea in a big glass jar with a spigot.

Luke appeared from the roof and set the table.

Annie woke up and, looking dazed, headed toward the deck gripping her midsection. "What's that garlicky smell?"

"Lunch." He lifted the lid and pulled the tray of perfectly seasoned walleye fillets off the grill. "Luke and I caught these last night."

Annie's face went pale. No. More like ashen-green. He'd seen that same skin color when rookies got seasick on the lakes. She slapped a hand over her mouth and backed away. Fast. She didn't make it far before she retched in an empty flowerpot.

He set the fish back on the grill and bounded down the steps with a handful of napkins. "Wow, Annie, I'm sorry. I thought you'd like fish and didn't think…"

She breathed deep and held out her hand to stay back. "I'll be fine in a minute."

He watched her heave once more but nothing came out. He placed his hand on her back and held out the napkins.

She gripped his hand. Hard.

He suddenly chuckled at the situation. Who threw up in an empty flowerpot? "You done?"

"I don't know."

He caught his brother's eye. "Luke, grab a bottle of water, would you?"

Luke had filled his plate but stood frozen in place, eyes wide. Then he moved quickly, slamming the cooler lid and bounding down the stairs with water. "What's wrong with her?"

"No, don't…" Annie retched again.

Luke backed away. "Whoa…"

Matthew took the water bottle from his brother, no longer seeing the humor in this. "Do me a favor."

"Yeah?"

"Take my truck and go get your stuff. We'll finish the roof tomorrow." Matthew threw him his keys.

Luke caught them. "How will you get home?"

"Just do it." He didn't think Annie wanted an audience, and since she gripped his hand tighter than a vise, he wasn't going anywhere soon. Besides, he could walk the couple miles home if he had to.

"Okaaaay." His brother narrowed his gaze. "So, what's the deal here?"

"Go, will you?"

Luke nodded. He grabbed his plate on the way.

Matthew ignored the swishing sound of his brother getting a pop from the ice-filled cooler before finally leaving. He handed Annie the water bottle. "Here."

She shook her head, scattering tears. Her hand trembled in his as she lurched down and dry-heaved one more time.

Helpless, he rubbed her back.

"Ugh! Sorry," she mumbled and let go of him.

He noticed that her hands shook as she pushed back her hair. He poured water over the napkins and handed them to her.

She wiped her mouth and forehead then took a swig of water from the icy bottle. "Thanks."

He frowned. "Sorry about lunch."

"It's okay." She teetered a little. "I think I need to go inside. Maybe lie down."

Without asking, he scooped her up into his arms and headed for the sliding door to the laundry room.

She gasped. "I can walk."

"No way. You look like you might pass out."

"It'll pass." She burped. "Sorry."

"Hey, you're not going to get sick on me, are you?"

She was sipping water again and sort of giggled. "I'm not making any promises."

He tucked her head over his shoulder. "Point it that way, then."

She laughed. An awkward, embarrassed kind of laugh. "I'm so sorry."

"You! I'm the one who messed up. I should have asked you before I grilled fi—"

She quickly placed her fingers against his lips. "It's okay. Just don't mention that word again."

He playfully bit her fingers and then smiled at the surprised look on her face. "I won't."

She smiled back as he walked her into the living room and deposited her on the couch.

"Where's Luke?"

"I sent him home." He sat on the edge of a chair across from her. "Does your doctor know about you getting sick a lot?"

Annie looked away. "She said it's a good sign." Then a shadow fell across her face. She looked so small on the couch by herself.

"What is it?"

She shook her head.

"Talk to me, Annie. What else did the doctor say?"

Her eyes filled with tears. "I'm high-risk. There's no guarantee I can do this—"

He was out of the chair and next to her in an instant, drawing her into his arms.

She went limp and plunked her forehead against his shoulder. "I can't lose this baby."

He held her tighter. "You won't, Annie. I promise you won't."

She pulled away and sniffed. "You can't make that kind of promise."

He shushed her. "Yes, I can."

He didn't know what else to say. He'd shake the very earth to give her everything she needed. To make sure Jack's kid grew strong until birth and beyond.

Starting with food. "Did you eat anything today?"

"Some toast."

He gently pushed back her hair and kissed her forehead. "How about some eggs?"

"Matthew—"

"Look, I said I'd help and I mean it. I'm going to take care of you."

"But—"

"We're going to do this together. We're going to see to it this baby makes a strong appearance come November."

Her eyes grew wide. "Why?"

Feelings surfaced he couldn't examine or share. "Because I loved Jack like a brother, and that makes you my family, too."

Her eyes got all watery again. "I could use some good family."

That was a good dodge. He couldn't take more tears so he quickly stood. "Stay put and rest. I'll be right back."

Annie lay against the pillows and closed her eyes, willing the room to stop spinning. The sound of Matthew tinkering in the kitchen soothed. His words had, too, but not nearly as much as his embrace. How could that be? And what kind of woman did that make her?

She rubbed her forehead. She used to be capable of handling things on her own. Plowing through the pain of life, she dealt. It was one of the things Jack said he'd always admired about her. When had she become so needy? So weak?

There were so many things to fear these days, and hoping for the best got a person only so far. God seemed miles away, and yet Matthew was right here as he'd said. Strong and sweet Matthew with his promises. Promises she desperately wanted to cling to and believe.

She smelled melted butter and braced for the swell of nausea that didn't come. Instead, her stomach rumbled. The teakettle whistle blew and she smiled. He was making her tea again.

Ginger's words about caring for someone new filtered through the haze of her mind. If Matthew wasn't careful, he might steal part of her heart. But never the whole. Jack had that and always would.

Jack...

Minutes later, Matthew appeared with a plate of steaming scrambled eggs that had a liberal amount of black pepper and probably salt, too. Plus, a mug of tea. "Here."

She sat up, suddenly famished, and took the plate, inhaling the spicy, buttery scent.

He set her mug on the coffee table with a soft clunk.

Annie scooped a forkful of the fluffiest eggs into her mouth. "These are good."

He smiled. "I use water instead of milk. A trick our chef taught me."

"Oh." Jack had always said they ate well out on the lakes. Better than he did at home. He'd never bought into her idea of nutrition. She waited to see how that first bite would settle. When nothing happened, she ate more.

"Eggs are good for you. I'm glad you had some in the fridge. I'm thinking you need more protein and not just toast."

Annie nodded again. He was probably right. She ate eggs. Even some broiled chicken on occasion. And normally seafood, too. She closed her eyes a second. She couldn't even think about fish without her belly turning. "Can you do me a favor?"

"Sure."

"Can you take care of the grill before you leave? I don't think I can handle it." Annie finished the eggs and set her empty plate on the coffee table then leaned back to sip her tea.

"No problem."

"Thanks for making lunch, by the way." Her eyelids felt heavy again. She set down her tea with a tired sigh. Maybe a short nap before the only class she had scheduled today at three. All she did was sleep, it seemed.

She was supposed to feel more energy soon. Her doctor had explained that once she passed the three-month mark, she'd feel better. And stronger. She needed all the strength she could get and was already a week past that fourteen weeks mark.

"You're welcome." Matthew's voice sounded soft and low.

Surely, he'd leave soon.

"When's your next doctor appointment?"

"Next month." Matthew might be gone by then. Back on the lakes.

"I want to go with you."

She shifted and stared. "You're serious."

He smiled, standing tall and solid in front of her. "Yup."

"Do you realize what that might look like? People will talk."

"I don't care about that and neither should you. It will look like a friend supporting another friend." He gave her a wink. "No worries, okay?"

She sighed, too tired to argue. "I guess if you're still around."

"I'm glad you see things my way." He grinned.

His way?

What was he talking about? This wasn't a debate. But then she'd caved on the heels of him winning the roof argument. How many battles might they have in the name of him helping her? Would she always give in so easily? The possibilities exhausted her but a zip of anticipation shot through her, too.

Having Matthew's support wasn't unwelcome, but caring for him was another matter entirely. Ginger thought it was okay, but Annie knew it wasn't. Not in a small town like Maple Springs where she depended on her good name for business. Not with her in-laws who'd brand her disloyal or worse.

That scarlet letter burned a little hotter. No way would she let herself fall for Matthew.

Chapter Four

Matthew cleared away the remains of lunch and cleaned the grill. He disposed of the leftover fish then tied up the bag and threw it in the garbage can near the garage, far away from Annie. He also cleaned up the yard from any stray shingles before checking on her.

Annie hadn't moved from the couch.

Was that much sleeping normal? He stepped back outside onto the deck and looked up Ginger's store on his phone. He hit the connect button.

"Spice of Life, how can I help you?"

He could hear the ruckus of milling customers in the background, so he got to the point real quick. "Ginger? Matthew Zelinsky. Do you know Annie's class schedule today?"

"Ummm, let's see, on Fridays through the summer I think she has only one. A stretching class for a group of elderly folks from Sunrise Center. Is she okay?"

"She's out cold and I don't want to wake her. I'll give them a call."

"I don't know, Matthew—"

"Thanks." He disconnected.

Matthew wasn't looking for permission. Obviously,

Annie needed to rest. Falling asleep for the second time that day nailed that one home pretty clearly. Like it or not, he'd do whatever it took to take care of Annie and her baby.

He raked his hands through his hair and sat down on the deck steps. Staring at the backyard, he processed what he was doing and why.

He had his fill of responsibility at work. His list of duties made him want a simple life when it came to relationships. He'd never wanted to think much about anyone other than his crew, and pleasing his captain.

Things had changed after he'd kissed Annie. His simple life had changed when Jack died.

He bowed his head to pray, but the words wouldn't come. He didn't give God much room in his life these days, and he couldn't say he knew the reason. Lazy, maybe? He'd been raised in a faith-filled home and his parents had instilled the need to obey God from the get-go. But somewhere along the way, Matthew had taken over the wheel and put God aft deck. He'd tucked the Lord in the stern of his life.

As a first mate, Matthew was used to giving orders on the freighter. He had responsibilities on board. He couldn't expect to order Annie into line any more than he could expect to know what she needed or how to meet those needs. All he knew was that he'd stepped beyond feelings of mere friendship. Annie wasn't ready for that. Was he?

Matthew looked into the sky, hoping he did the right thing and then looked up Sunrise Center on his phone and called the number. His first priority was to make sure Annie rested. In moments, he found the person in charge of canceling the exercise class. He gave his name and number explaining simply that he was a friend of Annie's and that she couldn't make it in today due to illness.

Slipping his phone into the back pocket of his jeans, he stood, grabbed a bottle of water from the cooler and entered the house. Annie was bound to give him flack for this, but she'd have to understand he was trying to do the right thing. Jack would expect nothing less from him.

Annie woke with a start. She'd dreamt of Jack. Something she hadn't done the last few weeks. In fact, she'd gone almost a month without dreaming of her late husband. But moments ago, she'd been searching the house for him, opening doors and calling out his name, but he wouldn't answer. Why was Jack hiding from her? In her dream, she'd grown angrier with each door opened and then slammed until she'd felt ready to explode.

She heard a soft snore and quickly sat up, rubbing her eyes.

Jack?

No. She sucked in a deep breath, hoping to ease the ache in her chest, the disappointment. Waking up always hurt.

Matthew dozed in a chair near the window. A gardening magazine lay open on his lap. His sandy-brown hair tended to curl at the ends and looked messy. His jaw was rough with unshaved stubble and his chin dipped toward his chest.

He'd get a kink in his neck if she didn't wake him. Annie didn't move because the temptation to crawl into his lap nearly swamped her. It wasn't fair to lean on him so much. She shouldn't seek to assuage her pain with Matthew's comfort. Needing his gentle touch was becoming a habit and he'd only been home for a few days.

What happened when he left again? She needed to

cope on her own. Stand on her own. She'd done it before. She could do it again.

The mantel clock over the fireplace suddenly chimed four times. She'd slept for two and a half hours. And then it hit her. She had a movement class. Jumping up, she grabbed her purse and fished for her phone as she scurried into the kitchen so that Matthew wouldn't hear. She shouldn't care. He should have left by now. He should have woken her up, too.

"Hello, Carly? It's Annie Marshall. Is Sue— What? Oh, yes, I'm feeling better, thank you. Canceled? Who canceled my class? Oh, I see. Yes, yes, that was fine. He's a family friend. And please, give the group my apologies. I'll credit your monthly invoice. Thanks." She clicked her phone closed with a sharp snap.

"I called in for you." Matthew's voice sounded soft from behind her.

Anger from her dream still lingered. It didn't take much to reignite it like the catch of a lit match to newspaper.

"Annie? Did you hear me?"

She whirled on him. "You had no right to do that!"

"You were sleeping. For the second time today, I might add."

"So?"

"So, don't you think you needed the rest?"

He was in for a big surprise if he thought she'd let him play watchdog. "What I *need* is for you to mind your own business and leave me alone!"

She charged past him into the living room. Her emotions ran rampant. More hormones? She didn't care. Nobody messed with her schedule but her.

Matthew followed. "Maybe *you* are my business."

"Not if I don't want to be!" Without looking away

from his surprised face, Annie flung the front door open. "Out. Now."

A sudden knock on the screen door startled her. Startled them both. A pretty woman blushed furiously on the porch. "Uh, sorry, Annie Marshall?"

Annie clenched her fists. "Yes?"

"Umm, I'm Holly Miller from the Maple Springs Historical Society, do you have a minute? Or should I come back another time?" The woman had obviously heard her yelling.

The way Annie figured, inviting the girl in might actually push Matthew out. "No, no. Come in, please. He was just leaving."

But Matthew didn't budge. In fact, he looked amused, and that made her mad all over again.

Holly gave him an awkward wave. "Hi, Matthew."

"Holly." He nodded. "How's it going?"

"Pretty good. I take it you're home for the month?"

Annie held her breath before she blew steam. Great, they knew each other. Did they have to play catch-up now?

"I am."

"That's great." Holly cast a nervous glance her way.

Annie gestured toward the couch. "Please, have a seat. Can I get you some tea?"

"Oh, no, thank you. I came by to ask…" Holly glanced quickly at Matthew before she sat down. "If you'd be willing, that is, well the historical society would like to open an exhibit in honor of your late husband. We're planning the upcoming year's events and believe Memorial Day of next year might be a good choice."

Annie sat down, her smile frozen in place. That was a year away. Why'd she have to think about it now?

The girl took a breath and went on. "Considering that

Mr. Marshall donated several antiques over the years, we'd like to build a display from his maritime collection of the Northern Great Lakes area."

Maritime history and collecting anything to do with freighters and shipwrecks had been Jack's hobby. Shipping, both past and present, had been his passion.

"With your approval of course." Again, Holly glanced at Matthew before looking at her. "It can be a temporary or permanent donation."

"Of course." Annie wasn't sure what else to say.

In her heart, she knew Jack would be thrilled to have his area trinkets and charts on display. Stuff she'd teased him about collecting. Dust magnets, she'd called them. But she hadn't looked through any of that *stuff* since before he died.

Annie glanced at Matthew.

He rubbed his chin, but his gaze remained fixed on her. In his eyes, she read understanding. He knew her reservations. Probably knew her limitations, too. When had they learned to communicate without words?

Holly cleared her throat and then pulled out a business card from her demure little purse and handed it over. "Give it some thought. We have plenty of time. I'd be happy to help go over the considered items with you. Again, we're hoping to stay with a maritime history theme and anything you feel you can contribute will be greatly appreciated and tax-deductible if you choose to make a permanent donation."

Annie took the card and nodded, her voice trapped below the tightening of her throat.

Matthew stepped forward and extended his hand to the pretty young woman. "Thanks, Holly. She'll be in touch."

Holly took the cue for what it was. Shaking Matthew's

hand, she smiled at Annie. "Thank you for your time and please accept my deepest condolences for your loss."

Annie nodded again and managed a thick-sounding, "Thank you."

Matthew waited until Holly left. "I can help with that."

Annie shook her head. He'd helped enough. "No. No. I can do it."

"I know what to look for. While I'm here, we can take a quick peek and get it done. Then you'll know if you have enough for Holly to build an exhibit around."

Annie gritted her teeth. "Don't you have somewhere else to go? Like a date or something?"

He barked out a harsh laugh. "I'm not dating anyone." Then he teasingly bumped her with his elbow. "I'd rather spend time with you."

"You might want to rethink that." Annie ignored the flip in her belly and slumped back down in the chair.

Why wouldn't he go away already? She was glad he'd been here to deal with Holly from the historical society. Glad he'd offered to look over Jack's things, too. She hadn't been able to face them. But she didn't want to admit those things aloud.

He smiled. "Because you're grumpy when you wake up?"

"I'm not grumpy. I'm mad and with good reason, too."

"Maybe so."

Still, she might as well take Matthew up on his offer. Facing Jack's things wasn't something she looked forward to doing alone. Who better to help her than Matthew? He'd know what Jack would want donated.

"Jack's office is upstairs." Annie looked hesitant.

"I can check it out myself if you'd rather."

She lifted her chin. "I can do it."

He didn't think she could. Her eyes looked haunted and sad.

Matthew was glad he hadn't teased her about Holly Miller being the biggest gossip in Maple Springs. His presence here and their arguing was bound to spread around town. Annie didn't need the added pressure. Or worry. And he didn't want to get booted before going through Jack's stuff. He'd meant what he'd said. He liked spending time with her. Maybe more than he should.

When Annie marched toward the stairs, he followed.

There were two bedrooms and a bathroom at the top. He glanced into the room with an open door. Annie's bed took up a lot of space and the breeze blew in making the white gauzy curtains dance. The door leading to the room across the short hallway was closed. She stood in front of it, clenching and unclenching her hands.

"Have you been in here since Jack's death?"

"No."

At least she wouldn't be alone. He'd be with her, and maybe facing this together would be good for them both. He gently touched her shoulder. "I'm right behind you."

"Thanks." She grasped the doorknob and twisted, and then walked inside.

Matthew was struck by an overwhelming sense of his best friend. All of Jack's things lay waiting as he'd left them when they first shipped out, as if he'd be right back. The closet door was open a crack and full of his clothes. Jack had his own closet because Annie had "too much stuff." That's what Jack had said many times with a shake of his head. His wife and her clothes had kicked him to the spare room.

His bookshelf was stacked with Great Lakes maritime history and shipping journals among other hardcover books and even biblical tomes. Jack had been a man of faith. How many times had he given Matthew sound advice and offers of prayer?

An antique tall ship model that Jack had worked on over a couple of winters was on a shelf along with shipping-themed antiques Jack had picked up at various ports. A captain's pocket watch complete with an old shipping company name lay next to a pair of equally old spectacles. A couple of flasks and even a few antique charts of Lake Michigan rested on the end of that shelf.

Photos of their recent Lake Michigan dive lay scattered on an office table, as if Jack had planned to organize them during his time off. He'd never gotten the chance. Those underwater pictures looked creepy even though Matthew had been there when they were taken.

He picked up a couple of the glossy green-tinted photos and flipped through them. Jack had been an avid diver. "You never wanted to scuba dive the lakes?"

"No." Annie's voice sounded strained. She stood in the middle of the room taking it all in. "I don't like seeing boats like the ones you guys work on at the bottom of the lake."

Matthew couldn't blame her. It was a grim reminder of how fickle the Great Lakes could be. Some storms blew in without warning and caused all sorts of havoc. He'd been on a few of those high-seas rides and he'd rather not repeat the experience.

He stepped closer. "I think there's plenty here for an exhibit, don't you?"

Annie turned toward him with watery eyes. "Jack would like that, wouldn't he?"

"I think so."

She took a deep breath. "Then I'll do it."

"I'll help you put it together."

"Matthew—" A tear trickled down her cheek, but she brushed it away. "Thank you."

He reached for her hand, wrapping his fingers over hers.

When he felt her shoulders shake, he pulled her close and wrapped his arms around her. "It's going to be okay."

"Yeah? When?" She melted into him instead of pushing him away.

Her defeated slump made his gut tighten. He wanted to tell her soon, but couldn't make that promise. Instead, he patted her back. "In time, Annie, you'll see."

"I know, but—" Her voice sounded muffled against his shoulder.

"But what?"

She shrugged.

Matthew hugged her closer. "We're going to be okay, Annie."

She nodded and hung on.

Matthew felt her breaking down. She shed silent tears that soaked through his T-shirt and tore through his heart. He closed his eyes, willing the hurt to stop, but knew only time eased the soreness of loss.

Holding Annie, he thought about his mother's warning of vulnerability. It'd be so easy to kiss her. Too easy to let things happen that shouldn't.

He gently pulled away from her. "You okay?"

She sniffed and gave him a weak smile. "Yes."

He focused on her mouth and then wiped away a rogue tear that dangled from her jaw. He needed to get out of there. "I should go."

"Like hours ago." She laughed then. "Go home, Matthew, and do something fun, okay?"

He chuckled, too. "Moving Luke in isn't exactly what

I'd consider fun, but it needs to be done. I'll see you tomorrow when we finish up the roof."

She smiled. "Thanks. Thanks for everything."

His heart bled. "Sure, Annie, no problem."

Matthew hightailed it out of there before he forgot his promise to be a friend.

That evening, Annie went back upstairs with a couple big laundry baskets. The door to Jack's room remained open and not nearly as intimidating as before. Running her fingers through her late husband's shirts hanging in the closet, she knew she had to get rid of them.

Maybe now was as good a time as any.

Pulling a shirt off its hanger, Annie brought the fabric to her nose and sniffed. Nothing. Not even a faint scent remained of Jack. Time to let go of his clothes and put them in the upcoming rummage sale at church. And then clear out this room and make it into a nursery.

If everything goes all right.

Annie shook the shirt out with a snap, forcing her fears aside. She didn't want to think about the scary what-ifs. Not tonight. She folded the cotton button-down and then tossed it in the basket. She pulled out another one and did the same. It didn't take long to plow through the closet and then move onto the oak dresser. When she'd finished with Jack's clothes, she moved to his desk. It was a huge thing she'd never wanted, but Jack had found it at a barn sale north of town.

Opening each drawer, she chuckled at the few things he'd stowed away. Pictures from trips taken together, a stash of fun-sized candy bars and sermon notes. He hadn't filled the drawers. There was little to go through except for the product manuals he'd kept for his camera. She'd keep his fancy camera with the adjustable lenses. Jack had loved taking pictures and Annie vowed she'd learn to use it. With a baby on the way, she needed to prepare for the onslaught of photo taking that was sure to come.

Annie sighed. She'd take those photos alone.

No. Matthew would be there, too. When he could be. He was a good friend who wouldn't abandon her. But what if they could be more? Biting the inside of her lip, Annie remembered that kiss. Maybe something more than grief had bloomed between them. Was that even okay?

She blew out her breath and stood.

Not going there.

Right now, she wanted to go through Jack's things. She'd review those items for donation with Matthew's help at another time. She had a hunch there'd be plenty to give the historical society even after separating what to keep and what not to.

Looking around the room, Annie zeroed in on Jack's tall ship model. She had too many fond memories watching him build it to let that one go. Jack had been a man of patience and precision. When their child grew into adulthood, she'd pass on that ship. Only then would she let it go.

Tapping her fingers on Jack's thick leather-bound Bible, she knew it needed to go to his parents. He'd want that. Flipping through the pages, Annie smiled at the various scribbles in the margins. Jack wrote so many questions without answers and yet his faith had never wavered.

"Oh, Jack…" she whispered. "What if I can't carry this child or raise it right?"

Like her husband's scribbles, there was no answer. She didn't expect one. But then Matthew's words came back to her. Only, in her thoughts, it was Jack's voice she heard.

It's going to be okay.

Annie prayed that proved true.

Chapter Five

The next morning, Matthew slipped behind the wheel of his truck with a travel mug in hand.

"You never told me what happened with Annie." Luke climbed in the passenger seat. "Is she having a baby?"

Matthew took a sip of his coffee. "Yeah, but don't say anything. She hasn't told Jack's folks yet."

"So, Jack never knew he was going to be a dad before he died?"

"Nope." Matthew didn't need that grim reminder.

He'd been glad for the long walk home from Annie's yesterday while Luke had his truck. With their brother Cam gone, the place was his until Luke came by well after dinner to move in. Matthew had done a lot of thinking, but none of it brought him peace of mind.

Once Luke settled in, Matthew pushed thoughts of Annie aside and watched a Tigers game on TV with his little brother. They hadn't talked about much other than baseball.

"You've got a thing for her, don't you?"

Matthew took another sip as he thought about the question. There was no sense ducking the truth, but it was an itchy thing having feelings for a woman he'd known for years as Jack's wife. "I guess I do."

"Have you asked her out?"

Matthew laughed. What did Luke know? He was still in college where dating was easy and uncomplicated. "It's not that simple."

"Why not?" Luke chugged his bottled orange juice.

Matthew shrugged. "She's still grieving."

Luke mulled that statement over. Tipping his head he said, "If you two end up getting married, Mom will be geeked over a ready-made grandchild."

Matthew's stomach clenched. He hadn't thought specifically about marriage. He hadn't thought that far ahead. Why would he? But then, maybe he should. Annie wasn't someone to get involved with on a casual level. There was no breaking it off with her. He'd said he'd be there for the baby, and meant it. If that didn't sound like a commitment, then he was crazy. Definitely crazy.

He'd grown up with younger brothers and sisters. He'd even changed a few diapers in his day, but they were his siblings. Not his responsibility except for an hour or two of babysitting.

Luke had a point, though. Their mom's common complaint, right after voicing her disappointment that none of them had married, was no grandkids.

His brother Darren had gotten close. But after his fiancée took off with the best man, Darren had steered clear of women ever since. His other brothers were nowhere close to a serious relationship, and his sisters were even worse. Each one concentrated on their careers and callings that did not include potential husbands.

"You got it bad." Luke laughed.

"What?"

Luke laughed harder. "Dude, you went white as a sheet just now."

Matthew gave his brother a sharp look. "What do you know?"

His brother grinned. "Obviously, more than you."

Matthew had a sinking feeling that Luke might be right. He'd made promises to Annie without thinking it through. Gut-level commitments he wasn't ready for. But he owed Jack.

"Just get your tool belt and keep your mouth shut."

That made Luke grin even wider.

Exiting the truck, Matthew shook off his brother's comments. He might know Annie better than most, but that didn't make marriage their future. Jack had loved his wife, but his mother didn't exactly get along well with Annie and it used to drive Jack crazy.

That's what married people did. They drove each other crazy thinking of the others before themselves. He had enough of that on the freighter, making sure everyone got paid and had plenty to do on their shifts.

He clicked shut the driver's-side door and looked at the house. Was Annie feeling better or was she sick again this morning? How long would her nausea last? *That* drove him crazy. These constant thoughts and worry for her.

Luke slapped him on the shoulder and laughed again. "You look like you're about to face a firing squad."

A sick and cranky Annie was pretty close. She'd been something when she'd tried to kick him out yesterday. But then they'd gone over Jack's stuff. She'd been grief-stricken. No way could he simply *date* Annie Marshall. She loved her dead husband.

He followed his brother around to the backyard. He spotted Annie sitting on the deck, her head back and facing up toward the sun with her eyes closed. Yup, sick again. He took a deep breath.

"Take your time," Luke whispered.

Matthew nodded. How'd the kid get so smart? "Morning, Annie."

She opened her eyes and smiled. "Morning."

His pulse picked up speed. Dressed for work in navy leggings and an oversized light blue T-shirt, she looked pretty. And young. Despite the fine lines near her eyes, Annie Marshall hands-down beat a lot of women half her age.

She spotted Luke and waved.

He waved back before climbing the ladder.

Matthew stepped closer. "How are you feeling today?"

"Just a little nausea. I'll be fine, though. I even ate eggs for breakfast. With lots of salt and pepper like you made them. Go figure."

He smiled, feeling like he stood on the deck of a rocking ship without a railing. "Any classes today?"

Her gaze narrowed. "Don't even think about it, mister. I have two and I'm going."

He put his hands up in surrender. "Okay, okay. I'll check in later."

She rolled her eyes. "You don't have to check on me."

"I know." He reached in the cooler, grabbed two bottles of ice-cold water—Annie had added more ice—and then climbed up the ladder to join Luke.

He didn't *have* to check on her, but he would. He wanted to.

By the time Annie started the final relaxation stretch that announced the end of her last class for the day, she spotted Matthew stepping into her studio. He stood out like a weed in a garden. Tall and masculine, he held a ridiculously feminine bouquet of flowers in his hands.

He gave her a nod and sat down.

What did he think he was doing here with those?

Her clients were of various ages and skill levels, but today's class was filled with women and most of them young. It didn't take long for several to notice a good-looking man in their midst. Whispers started and heads turned.

"Remember to breathe. Eyes, closed. We've got a few minutes in this pose." Annie lay on her back on a mat in the front of the room. Her palms were flat open and positioned over her head. Her bare feet were apart, too, with feet flexed toward her body with toes in the air.

Talk about feeling vulnerable. She didn't dare look at Matthew again, even though she felt his gaze on her. Probably staring at her feet.

The next moments passed slowly. Agonizingly slow.

What was he doing here? She could get up and see, but that would only distract the class. The full body stretch was important after nearly an hour and half of concentrated movements.

"Okay, now breathe deeper. Slowly wiggle those fingers and toes. Bring your knees into your chest, keeping eyes closed. Continue to breathe deeply. When you're ready, sit up and we're done."

Annie heard the chatter grow louder as some rolled up the exercise mats they'd brought with them. Others wiped down her studio-provided mats with her home-made spray mixture of vinegar, borax and water.

She got up and cleaned her mat while Matthew spoke with a small circle of women he appeared to know in the waiting area. How many of them had he dated? He'd grown up in Maple Springs. There'd be women he'd gone out with still around, right?

She didn't want to think about any of that. She had no claim on Matthew Zelinsky. In all the years she'd known him, he didn't want to be claimed. Matthew had made no secret of his desire to remain single.

She glanced at the group. Several ladies eyed that bouquet with interest. She threw on her T-shirt and checked her watch. Jack's mom planned to stop by in half an hour.

Annie had Jack's Bible to give her and then they'd grab lunch. Time spent with her mother-in-law might be a good thing, even if her nerves didn't agree.

Matthew's presence didn't help. And neither did this new jittery feeling she had when around him.

She finally walked toward him. "Hello."

Matthew slipped out of the circle of females and held out the bundle of flowers. "These are for you."

Annie forced a smile. "Thanks."

The conversation of the circle stilled.

Great, just great! That'd get the rumor mill started for sure. Annie took the blooms calmly enough, but her heart bounced around her rib cage. Maybe she'd come out of that final stretch too soon.

"I'll put these in water." Annie turned toward her office, and her stomach dropped when Jack's mom entered the studio. For a minute she stood mute, blinking like a kid caught with her hands in the cookie jar before dinner.

Of course, her mother-in-law tended to be early. Why would today be any different? "Marie!"

Her mother-in-law looked confused before controlling her features into that pinched expression Annie knew all too well. "Lovely flowers."

"Yes." She wanted to run.

The circle of women broke up and several had left.

Most of her class had gone, with only a couple of stragglers left talking in the corner.

"The roof is done. And the debris Dumpster is also gone." Matthew stepped close and took the flowers from her fingers. Giving her hand a quick squeeze, he whispered, "You're going to crush these if you hold them any tighter."

Annie clenched her teeth and silently counted.

Marie Marshall glanced from Matthew to her, to the flowers and then back to her. Her dark eyes simmered with hurt and something close to disgust.

Annie could only imagine what her mother-in-law must be thinking. By the look in the woman's eyes, it wasn't good. But Annie hadn't done anything wrong.

"Marie, you remember Matthew Zelinsky, Jack's first mate on the freighter. He and his brother replaced my roof this week."

Matthew held out his hand. "Mrs. Marshall. How are you and your husband?"

Marie hesitated, quickly shook Matthew's hand and then let go. "We're holding up."

Matthew smiled, seemingly unfazed by the woman's frostiness. "Jack was a good man. Like another brother to me."

Marie nodded, clearly not in the mood for this kind of small talk.

Annie made fists. How dare she treat Matthew like he was somehow beneath her concern! They'd all lost Jack and they all hurt from it.

Matthew raised the bouquet toward her. "I thought these might cheer you up. I'll put them in water and get going." Then he gave Jack's mom a wide smile. "Good to see you, Mrs. Marshall. Take care."

The couple of clients hanging around finally walked toward the door. One of them waved. "Thanks, Annie."

"See you next week." She waved back. Then to Jack's mom, she said, "Marie, why don't you have a seat while I get my bag."

The woman looked around with distaste. "I'll stand by the door."

Of course Marie wouldn't sit down. That might be construed as giving her approval, and Jack's mom had never approved of anything Annie did. Not her career choice, her studio, the way she dressed, wore her hair or what she chose to eat. All of it had garnered that pinched look for the past fifteen years.

It was a wonder that Jack's parents had guaranteed her business loan with the equity on their house. But then, Jack had persuaded them, and Annie promised to have the loan paid off sooner than later. Too bad that *sooner* came in a way none of them would have expected. Once Jack's death benefit came in, she'd pay off the loan. But she'd never be done with her in-laws. Not when she carried their grandchild.

"I'll only be a moment." Annie slipped away into her small office as Matthew was setting the flower-filled vase on her desk.

"I clipped the ends." How many men knew to do that to the ends of fresh flowers?

Annie stuck her face into the bouquet and breathed deep the sharp fragrance of daisies mixed with soft yellow roses. "These are beautiful. Thank you."

"I thought so." Matthew gently wiped the tip of her nose with his finger. "Daisy dust."

Annie let loose a nervous giggle and scrubbed her nose.

He stared at her a moment before looking beyond her. "You want a bodyguard?"

Annie glanced at the entrance where Marie stood with a forbidding frown on her face. That'd throw her mother-in-law for a loop, but having Matthew along was the last thing she needed and one more thing for Marie to disapprove of.

She reached for her purse and the bag with Jack's Bible and a few other things Marie might want. "No. But thanks for the offer."

He touched her arm, sending a shiver through her. "I stopped by to ask if you'd like to come to my parents' place on Memorial Day for a cookout."

Annie shook her head. She wanted to go to Jack's grave and doubted she'd be good company. She wasn't up for a family gathering, anyway. "Thanks for the kind offer, but I'm going to pass."

He searched her eyes. "Call me if you need anything, okay?"

"I will." She meant it this time.

He gave her shoulder a soft squeeze and Annie nearly leaned into him. Without another word, he left.

She heard him say goodbye to Jack's mom with warm words of encouragement. Running her fingers over the flowers he'd given her, Annie squared her shoulders. She could do this. For her baby's sake and Jack's, she'd treat Marie with a little grace. Grief wasn't easy for anyone.

Plastering on a smile she didn't feel, Annie met her mother-in-law at the door. "Ready?"

Marie acted as if she couldn't exit the building quickly enough.

Annie locked up for the rest of the weekend. "Where would you like to go for lunch?"

Her mother-in-law looked her up and down. "Aren't you going to change clothes?"

Annie had pulled on a pair of gym pants over her leggings. Her T-shirt might be baggy, but it was perfectly acceptable. She glanced at her mother-in-law, who dressed in her usual long denim skirt and sweater set looking like she stepped out of an earlier era. The woman even wore dainty pearls. "I hadn't planned on it. I know a great little soup-and-sandwich shop a block over."

Marie let loose a sigh. "Okay, then."

They walked the short block without speaking, but then the noise of local teens hanging out and the bustle of shopping tourists made conversation a moot point.

Once seated, with their orders given, Marie finally got down to what had been on her mind. "Are you seeing that young man?"

Annie choked on her iced tea. "What?"

"Jack's first mate."

Marie knew his name. Why didn't she use it? "*Matthew* is a friend. He's been a friend to Jack and me for years. Why should that change?"

Her mother-in-law sat back. Her mouth worked into a grim line before she answered. "Because you're a widow now. And quite a bit older than he. Think of Jack. It doesn't look right for a *Christian* widow to be out carrying on."

Annie's mouth dropped open, but nothing came out.

Was she supposed to walk around in a black veil? Might be better if she let that one go without commenting. It wouldn't come out right, anyway.

Annie jammed her hands in her bag until her fingers felt the soft leather-bound Bible. She handed it over. "I thought you and John might like to have this."

Marie's eyes widened as she took it and leafed through the pages. "But this is Jack's Bible."

Annie set the bag containing one of Jack's college sweatshirts, a pair of binoculars she knew her in-laws could use to watch birds and some other small items at Marie's feet. "I think he'd like you to keep it."

Marie's eyes filled with tears. "But won't you miss it?"

Annie smiled, her heart softening. She had something far more precious from Jack. When the time was right, when she was sure the baby was strong and healthy, she'd let Jack's parents in on her news. But not yet. Not until she was sure.

"If I do, maybe I can swing by your house and ask to read it."

Marie looked surprised. As she should. Annie didn't make a habit of popping in to visit her in-laws. But that was bound to change with a baby to share with grand-parents.

And she'd have to share.

Her mother-in-law patted her hand in a rare gesture. "This will always be available to you."

Annie flipped her hand over to grip Marie's for a moment. She had to remember how difficult this must be on her, losing her only son. Her only child. "Thanks."

Marie squeezed and didn't let go. "Annie, I'm worried about you."

"Why?"

"You're working like nothing happened, scheduling more classes for summer. And then a younger man brings you flowers in front of everyone. In front of me."

Annie pulled her hand back. Hadn't she worried about that, too? What if other people in town judged her by how she mourned her husband's death? "My studio is my livelihood. People don't quit their jobs when they experience death. Take a leave, sure, but I already did that."

"For only two weeks. Do you really think that was enough time?"

Annie had been itching to get out of her house and

back to classes. Back to a sense of normal. "Enough time for whom?"

Marie got that pinched expression again.

Their food arrived and the subject was dropped. But it nagged at Annie like a rosebush thorn stuck in her skin. She winced at the image of Matthew handing her those flowers.

Wiping her mouth with a napkin, Marie sighed. "Don't you have girlfriends?"

"Yes, I do." But summer was Ginger's busiest time at the store. She didn't expect her friend to drop everything so she could hold Annie's hand.

"And do they bring you flowers?" Marie's eyebrows rose.

Annie saw where this was going and thought hard before answering. Had Ginger ever brought her flowers? Some of the women from church had, but those were sent via a florist and didn't really count.

The image of a yellow rosebush Ginger had given her jelled into certainty. *Yellow.* The color of friendship. Like the flowers Matthew had given her. And Annie smiled.

"Yes. Sometimes they do."

The morning of Memorial Day, Matthew looked out the kitchen window and snarled. Dreary, drizzly rain slid down the glass in thin streaks. He hoped it cleared up so they could picnic outside and play horseshoes.

"Glad we got that roof done." His brother slapped him on the shoulder.

Matthew yawned and nodded.

Surrounded by noisy men most of the year on a freighter, Matthew remembered why he'd moved in with Cam. Cam was rarely home when he was and vice versa. But peace and quiet had eluded him since his kid brother had moved in. He was over the TV on high volume and constant phone calls.

Luke dribbled milk over the side of his cereal bowl and left it on the table. The kid was a slob, too.

Matthew clenched his jaw. Used to room inspections and the like during his maritime academy days and even on the freighter, Matthew had learned tidy habits. Jack Marshall had demanded a neat and clean ship.

"Are you going to wipe that up?" he asked the retreating form.

"I'll get to it when I put the bowl in the sink." Luke slouched onto the couch. With nowhere but their parents' house to go this *fine* Memorial Day, Luke's live-wire energy had fizzled out.

"Dishwasher," Matthew corrected and rinsed a dishcloth. He wiped away the cereal crumbs and milk puddles from the small table.

"Whatever," Luke mumbled around a mouthful.

"I'll meet you at Mom and Dad's." He was showered and dressed with no reason to hang around.

Luke raised his spoon in acknowledgment. Out with friends until late the night before, his little brother ran much slower than normal this morning.

In his truck, Matthew drove north toward his family's home. Passing by the Maple Springs cemetery, he noticed the fresh floral wreaths and American flags that had been placed with care in honor of the day.

He spotted a small car that looked like Annie's parked near a grove of trees and slowed down. Contemplating turning in at the next drive, Matthew pulled off the road instead. If Annie was there, he doubted she'd want him intruding at Jack's grave site.

He scanned the area. Their town's cemetery was good-sized, with driveways leading to walkways that twisted and turned through woods and open fields. There weren't many people there this morning perhaps because of the drizzle. But then somebody had placed all those wreaths. The town maintenance folks had probably staked in the flags.

He watched a lone, slight figure holding an umbrella with one hand, while the other flew through the air in conversation. It was Annie.

Talking...

To Jack.

He gripped the steering wheel as she paced back and forth. Whatever she said, Jack was getting an earful. Annie looked agitated. Animated. And incredibly lovely.

Matthew wondered if his friend and captain was up in Heaven listening. And if Jack could hear her, what might he say in return? What advice would he give his widow?

He swallowed around the lump in his throat and checked the rearview mirror. He pulled back out onto the road and headed for his folks' house. Lost in images of Annie at Jack's grave, it didn't take long before Matthew pulled into his parents' driveway.

His mom spotted him the minute he walked in the door. "Matthew. You're here early, and where's Annie?"

"She decided not to come." His throat felt tight when he said it. He couldn't get the image of her talking to her husband's grave out of his mind.

She touched his shoulder. "Maybe you can call her later."

He nodded. But maybe he wasn't in the mood for family and horseshoes and a campfire. He wanted to head over to Annie's and make sure she was all right. But that'd have to keep. The woman deserved time to grieve in her own way. She'd promised to call him if she needed anything.

"You okay, honey?"

The heaviness of missing his friend lay like a heavy cloak dragging on the ground. "Yeah, I'm fine."

He nearly laughed at how he'd echoed Annie's own words. Those two little words were often a shield. *I'm fine* meant the opposite. A *no-trespass* sign for the soul.

His mom wrapped her arms around his waist. "Come in and tell me what's on your mind. I just made a pot of fresh coffee."

Matthew smiled. He smelled coffee mixed with the scent of slow-cooked ribs that would be thrown on the grill later. This was where he needed to be right now. There was something about coming home that seemed to make everything better. Annie didn't have that. With Jack gone, going home for her meant entering an empty house.

He'd call later and see about bringing her back out. He sensed that she needed family now more than ever. If he could provide that for her, to get her through, he'd do it. He'd become Annie's family. All he had to do was convince her that it was okay to accept the invitation.

Chapter Six

Salty tears mixed with the foggy drizzle that surrounded Annie, making her whole face wet. She folded the umbrella and laid it at her feet. She didn't care about the damp. She didn't care about the chilled air that probably chased many away from the Memorial Day parade progressing down Main Street. She heard the drums played by the high school marching band in the distance. The cheerful rhythm might as well be a buzzing mosquito.

She stared at Jack's modest gravestone with the inadequate description, *Favored son and good husband.* Had she really approved that? Her in-laws had picked it out. At the time, Annie didn't make a fuss because who really cared about gravestones?

Staring at the hunk of stone that was severe and plain, just like Jack's parents, she realized she'd made an error. She should have picked out something more elaborate. Jack would have gotten a kick out of a mermaid or something equally frivolous.

"What am I supposed to do, Jack? Stop seeing him?"

She didn't expect an answer. Jack had never answered her right away. He'd look at her with his dark eyes that saw everything and let her rant. "He's our friend. And a good friend, too. He replaced the roof and he's helping me cope. Why can't I see him?"

She paced some more, reliving Marie's horrible words over and over. Labeled a widow, was she supposed to stop living because her husband was dead? Shut off contact with the only person who knew Jack as well as she did?

"I kissed him. Was that wrong?" Annie plunked down on the wet grass. She didn't care that her jeans were getting soaked through. Jeans she couldn't even button. She'd left the top undone and the zipper bit into her skin, so she shifted.

Reliving that kiss shared with Matthew only a week after Jack went into this spot of earth made her even more uncomfortable. That's what made seeing Matthew dangerous. One kiss had stirred up a tempest. A storm that still raged.

"I felt alone. Really alone, and Matthew understood. He knew I needed warmth. Some kind of real contact, you know?"

Maybe these feelings she had for Matthew were her hormones taking over. Her changing hormones that kept her baby safe made her feel an attraction that shouldn't be there.

It was simply too soon.

Running her fingers over the cold stone, she lowered her head. "Why'd you die?"

It had been two and a half months since she'd said goodbye to her husband before he'd boarded ship, never to return again alive. There wasn't a day that she didn't feel Jack's absence in her life. But lately, her thoughts were filled with Matthew, too.

"Oh, Jack, I'm so confused."

Pray.

Annie didn't hear the word, she felt it. "No."

God had left her pregnant and widowed.

Pray.

Annie shook her head against the sound of Jack's voice in her mind. She didn't want to. She didn't want to need to pray. She didn't want to *need*. But tears flowed down her cheeks and the now familiar upheaval in her stomach churned and gurgled.

"God, please…" It was all she could manage.

If what she'd heard at church was true, then God knew her heart better than she did. Maybe He'd understand that she didn't know how to pray anymore much less know how she *should* feel.

"Please…"

"Why don't you call her?" His mom covered the bowl of her homemade pierogies with plastic wrap. "See if she'd like to come out for a campfire. I have all these leftovers. She can take some home."

Looking over the leftover BBQ ribs and chicken, Matthew shrugged. "She's not much of a meat eater."

"Then take her some salads." She lifted the bowl. "Take her these. I filled them with cheese and potatoes or sauerkraut and onion. No meat."

"Are you trying to get rid of me?"

"No need." Helen Zelinsky laughed. "You've been far away today."

Matthew loved the way his mom laughed. It bubbled up like a spring of happiness from within and flowed out over the whole family. His mother's laughter forced a smile in return, even though he didn't feel like smiling. Even though he'd spotted concern in his mom's eyes.

She patted his back. "You've been moping all day. Are you sure you're okay?"

He couldn't use the weather as an excuse. The morning drizzle had stopped when the sun made its appearance. The remaining fog burned off quickly, too. The afternoon climb up to summertime temperatures made him wish he'd worn shorts instead of jeans.

The clang of thrown horseshoes could be heard outside as well as more laughter. The Zelinskys knew a few things when it came to food and the game of horseshoes. He should be outside enjoying himself instead of in the kitchen helping his mom put away leftovers. He shouldn't be thinking about Annie, but he couldn't stop.

She'd looked so upset at Jack's grave. Of course, she was. Her husband was dead. Matthew clenched his jaw. Why'd he feel the need to rescue her from this sorrow he also felt? Grief was natural. Even needed. He should let her process her sadness and get some closure.

"I'm fine." But he grabbed his phone from his back pocket.

And his mom smiled at him.

He called Annie and walked into the next room.

"Hello?"

Hearing her voice did something to him. Tamping down nerves he hadn't experienced since he was a teenager, Matthew cleared his throat. "Hey, Annie."

"Matthew?"

"My mom has all these leftovers, including her killer pierogies. Are you going to be around? I can drop them off."

"Yeah, sure. I'll be here." She sounded fine. Perfectly fine. How'd she manage that after looking like a whirlwind at the cemetery?

"Great, I'll see you within the hour." He disconnected but didn't move. He stared out the windows, not really seeing the green of trees and lawn that framed the small sandy beach.

"Is she okay?" His mom walked into the family room where he stood.

"She sounded good." Matthew turned. "Do you think I could borrow your garden tiller?"

His mom looked puzzled. "Sure. It's in the barn. What for?"

"Annie's garden hasn't been tilled yet. Can you box up those leftovers while I load my truck? I'm going to head over there now."

His mom didn't question him, but he could tell she wanted more information. No doubt, she'd prefer that he bring Annie here instead of going there, but she didn't say that. She didn't have to. "I'll get it ready."

He pulled his mom into a bear hug. "Thanks."

She gave him a hard squeeze. "Be careful."

"Always."

After he'd loaded and secured the tiller in the bed of his truck, Matthew returned to the kitchen. He grabbed the box his mom had prepared and shifted it to get a better grip. "Whoa, what have you got in here that weighs a ton?"

"Just some syrup." His mom walked him out.

Matthew bent and kissed her cheek before climbing behind the wheel.

"Where are you going?" Luke tapped the truck's hood.

"To till up Annie's garden."

Luke didn't look surprised and grinned. "Coming back?"

"Maybe."

"Darren needs to get beat at horseshoes."

"Right." Matthew laughed. No one bested their older brother, except for their dad. And when the two teamed up? Forget it. He waved as he backed out of the driveway.

Maybe he could get Annie to come back with him for the campfire as his mom had suggested. They could throw a few shoes, roast some marshmallows—and then what? Cuddle by the fire? The idea appealed, but didn't seem right.

Matthew needed to get a handle on what he was doing and why fast. This had to be about helping Annie get through a rough time. This had to be about friendship.

Anything more had to wait.

But waiting was the last thing he wanted to do when he pulled into Annie's driveway and saw her standing on the porch. Her hair was loose and full. Golden. He wanted to take her into his arms and kiss away the worry lines that hugged her mouth.

"What's that for?" She met him at the sidewalk and pointed at the back of his truck.

He hoisted the box of leftovers. "Your garden."

Her eyes widened. "That's leftovers?"

"My mom sent syrup, too."

"Nice." She hurried to open the door for him.

He walked into the kitchen and set the box on the table. "You haven't rented a tiller yet, have you?"

"No." She peered into the box and pulled out a half-gallon-sized bottle of Zelinsky Syrup. "Wow. This will last me a while. I love your family's syrup."

"I know. Jack bought a bottle every Christmas."

She looked at him and her eyes filled with tears.

And Matthew felt like an idiot for reminding her. "I'm sorry."

"It's okay." She sniffed and then laughed. It was a bitter sound. "No Jack this Christmas."

Matthew's stomach tightened into a knot. "I know."

"At least I'll have syrup, right?" Annie forced a cheerful voice as she pulled out the foil-wrapped packages and opened one. "Let's see what we have here."

Matthew frowned as he watched her struggle for composure.

Then she grimaced at the BBQ ribs. "These will have to go home with you." Annie wrapped it back up and moved onto another foil package containing grilled chicken and then pierogies. "But these look great. I'll have this a little later."

Matthew watched her go through the box. Despite the smiles and cheerful voice, she wasn't fine. "My mom makes great homemade pickles. There's a jar of those, too."

"Tell your mom thanks for me." Annie put away the leftovers into her fridge. "Do you want anything to drink? Iced tea?"

"Not now." Matthew headed for the sliding glass door leading to the back deck. "I'm going to take a look at your garden. With this morning's rain, the soil will be perfect for tilling."

Annie stopped him with the touch of her hand on his arm. "You don't have to do this."

He looked down at her fingers. She wore a gold wedding band with a square-cut diamond in its center. Annie belonged to Jack and always would. Forcing his hands to remain at his sides, he nodded. "I know."

"But I haven't bought any plants or seeds. I thought maybe I'd pass on a garden this year."

"You'll regret that come summertime." Matthew reached for a wavy strand of her golden hair. Lifting it, his fingers grazed her skin above the wide neckline of her top.

He felt her tremble.

"You're probably right." Her voice sounded raw.

Matthew rubbed her hair with his thumb a moment more before letting go. Before he pulled her close. "I'll get to it, then."

* * *

Annie watched Matthew walk outside into the sun-drenched backyard and let out a ragged breath. That wasn't compassion she'd read in his eyes. Matthew struggled with the same attraction as she.

She ran shaking fingers through her hair as Ginger's words about caring for someone new whispered through her thoughts once again. But it was too soon. Much too soon to go there.

Matthew was right about the garden, though. She'd want fresh veggies come August when she had more energy and would need to eat more. But that didn't make it right to let him do all the work.

Annie stepped onto the deck as Matthew came around the corner hauling a small garden tiller. It was bigger than the electric one she usually rented.

As if sensing her watching him, he looked up and smiled.

"Why are you doing this?"

He shrugged.

"I don't like watching you do something I usually do for myself."

He grinned. "Then don't. Go in and fix a couple of plates so we can picnic when I'm done."

Annie wanted to argue but in the end, went inside. What was the point? Matthew seemed determined to do things for her. So maybe she should let him. Besides, she could definitely eat. Dinnertime rolled close and her stomach growled to be fed.

In the kitchen, Annie unwrapped the leftovers and made two plates. Ribs for Matthew, chicken for her. She snitched a quick bite before placing both in the microwave. The pierogies and broccoli slaw were stacked in plastic containers. There was more than enough for both of them. It looked like her dinner plans the following night were taken care of, too.

Rinsing off her fingers, she glanced out the window over the sink. Matthew tilled the small garden plot easily enough. The muscles of his arms were taut as he controlled the gas-powered tiller. And he was nearly done.

She set the microwave on a low reheat setting and fixed a couple of glasses of iced tea. Loading everything they'd need on a tray, Annie returned to the back deck and set the table. By the time the microwave beeped, Matthew had finished.

He headed for the laundry room to wash up. "Hey, I think I might have lost my watch. It's got a brown leather band. If you find it let me know."

"Okay." Annie brought both plates outside and set them on the table. "Perfect timing."

"Thanks." Matthew sat down and bowed his head.

"Could you say that out loud so it covers me, too?" She scooted into her chair and folded her hands in her lap.

He didn't look like he wanted to. "It's my family's mealtime prayer."

"That's fine." Annie closed her eyes and waited.

Matthew quickly recited the prayer. His voice sounded deep and sure as he repeated the rhythm of words that comforted like worn-in leather.

And these, Thy gifts…

Annie thought about that. Her baby was a gift she hoped to open with good health. Would he look like Jack? She hoped so. Pictures wouldn't ever be enough to remember her husband, but watching their son grow into someone who resembled his father would help. Wouldn't it?

When had she started thinking of her baby as a boy? *God gave gifts.*

Matthew's friendship was a gift, too. One she shouldn't throw away merely because she was a widow now. But she'd have to follow some rules. She needed to protect their friendship even though they missed the person who'd brought them together.

"You okay?"

Realizing Matthew had long since stopped praying, Annie looked up. "Oh. Yeah. Sorry."

He covered her hand with his. "I saw you at the cemetery this morning. If you need to unload, feel free."

She felt her eyes widen. He'd seen her? "I go there sometimes. You know—" Annie stopped. It would sound crazy to say when she needed to talk to him. "Just because. Have you been there?"

Matthew pulled his hand back and shook his head. "No. Not since the funeral."

Maybe she was morbid to feel closer to Jack there, where his body lay beneath four feet or so of earth. She knew his spirit was with God, but there was something final, a sense of closure perhaps, by talking to Jack next to his ridiculously plain grave stone.

"Next time, feel free to stop." Annie took a bite of chicken, wondering why she'd offered an invitation. She would not have wanted Matthew there this morning.

"Do you go often?"

She couldn't tell whether he thought that was odd or not, but he looked concerned. "Sometimes."

"Have you thought about talking to someone?"

Annie leaned back in her chair and laughed. "I am talking to someone. I'm talking to you."

He didn't see the humor in that.

This time, she covered his hand and gave it a squeeze. "I've spoken with my pastor and that was okay. I don't know. Maybe it's having gone through this before when my parents died, or my age. Whatever, but really what's anyone going to tell me? Or do? Jack's gone and he's not coming back. I'm dealing."

He nodded.

"What about you?"

He turned his hand over and held hers. "I don't know, Annie. My best friend's gone and there's this hole in me. I thought being with you, helping out where I can, might fill it."

"But it doesn't." She threaded her fingers through his.

"No. It doesn't."

She focused on the contours of his hand, feeling the rough spots of his palm. She built up the courage to finally ask what had plagued her for months. "How'd he look when you found him?"

Matthew took a deep breath and let it back out. "He looked peaceful. I thought he was asleep at first but knew that couldn't be. Jack never overslept on duty."

Annie closed her eyes, grateful for that. "No. He wouldn't."

"It was quick at least."

She looked into Matthew's face. His eyes had filled with tears, too. "I'm sorry you found him."

"Tough image to shake." His voice was barely above a whisper.

Annie went to him. Wrapping her arms around his shoulders, she felt him tense and then relax. It was an awkward embrace with her stooping down to meet him where he sat. But he quietly held onto her and tucked his face into her neck.

"We're going to be okay, you and I," she whispered.

He nodded but didn't speak. Maybe he couldn't.

She held on until it hurt. Letting go, she stepped back and stretched.

He let out a soft laugh that made more tears slip out and run down his cheeks. "Sorry. I should have pulled you onto my lap."

Her own eyes watery, she gave him a soft shove before sitting back down. "I'm glad you didn't."

They ate in companionable silence until Annie heard the voice she knew well coming from inside the house.

Her mother-in-law.

Marie Marshall called out again. "Annie? Are you home?"

Annie looked at Matthew and rolled her eyes.

He raised his eyebrows. "Aren't you going to answer?"

She scrunched up her nose. "Maybe she'll go away."

He shook his head but chuckled. "Nice."

Annie got up and opened the screen of the slider. "We're out here, Marie. Oh, and John. Hey, come on out and join us."

"We brought you some cake." Marie carried a small box and stopped when she saw Matthew standing near the table. Her lips thinned as she scanned their dinner plates.

Annie pulled out a chair. "John, this is Matthew Zelinsky, Jack's friend and first mate."

Her father-in-law gave him a ready smile and extended his hand. "Yes, yes, Matthew. The man whose family lives on a small lake that's perfect for ice fishing. How are you?"

Annie recalled that Jack had taken his dad on one of those jaunts up to the Zelinsky maple syrup farm. She'd never gone other than to pick Jack up. Annie had never been one interested in freezing on the ice waiting for fish to bite. Plus, she'd always had classes at the studio in the afternoons and the guys liked to make a whole day of it right into evening.

"Holding up. And you, sir?"

John nodded once. Understanding Matthew immediately. "Not easy, son."

"No. It's not."

When John said nothing more, Annie asked, "Can I get either of you some food? Matthew's mom sent enough for a small army."

"No, no, we've already eaten." Marie gripped the box tight. "We came over to put flowers on Jack's grave and thought we'd stop."

"Thank you. Would you like hot tea, then?" Annie offered.

"But you've got company." Marie's inflection on the last word was sharp. Sarcastic, even.

"Oh, I'll be on my way. I dropped off leftovers and tilled Annie's garden. My work's done here." Matthew hadn't missed Marie's tone, either. It was no wonder he wouldn't stay.

John smiled at her. "I'm glad you're going to have a garden this year. I'd sure miss those tomatoes."

Annie could have hugged her father-in-law. "Thanks to Matthew, you'll get them."

"Well, good. Cut that cake, Marie." John looked at Matthew. "Stay for cake. It's from the bakery by us that Annie likes."

Annie smiled. She usually brought a box of baked goods with her when she visited Jack's parents. Bribery by sweets, Jack had called it. That bakery was John's favorite, not hers.

Without a word, Marie went back inside to the kitchen.

"Okay." Matthew sat down.

"How's your new captain working out?"

Annie gave Matthew a grateful smile and gathered up their dinner plates and went into the kitchen.

Marie's rigid back faced her.

Annie filled the teakettle and set it on the stove, turning up the heat.

"You seem to be spending a lot of time with this man."

Annie clenched her jaw and counted to three before exhaling. "His name is Matthew and he's Jack's best friend."

"Was." Marie sliced the cake with force.

"Yes." Annie couldn't win this one. "He *was*."

Marie turned around, big knife in hand. "I'm not trying to tell you how to live your life, but—"

"Then don't," Annie snapped.

Marie pressed her lips into a tight line, as if weighing her next words. "As a Christian widow, you shouldn't be here with him all alone."

"He came to till my garden, Marie." Annie gestured toward the backyard. "And we ate outside."

Marie turned around and cut another piece of cake.

Annie looked out on the deck. Matthew and John conversed comfortably enough, but then her father-in-law had always been softer than Marie. Easier.

She grabbed a small stack of dessert plates from the cupboard. "I understand your concern, really I do. I know this isn't easy for you, either."

The knife slammed down on the counter. "You can't know what it's like to lose my only child."

Annie closed her eyes. Having never been a mother, that statement was true. But she had a hunch. Already loving the small person growing inside, Annie understood Marie's loss even if she couldn't feel it fully.

She touched her mother-in-law's shoulder. "I'm sorry."

The woman sniffed and shook off her touch. "Here, I'll take those plates and forks. You bring the tea."

Annie let her shoulders slump. There was no winning with her. But like swallowing a bitter pill, Marie might be right about being here alone with Matthew. The way he'd touched her hair, the way her breath had caught at the look in his eyes only enforced how dangerous the attraction they danced around was.

Annie was old enough to know the possible pitfalls ahead, but was she wise enough to steer clear? Sometimes she felt as if she walked in a dream, not knowing what felt real or imagined. Either way, she needed to tread carefully.

Very carefully where Matthew was concerned.

Chapter Seven

The next morning, Annie shifted Holly Miller's business card between her fingers. The Maple Springs Historical Society took first errand on her list of things to do today. She'd dressed with care, choosing a loose pair of cotton pants with a drawstring. Her middle was definitely thickening with a barely detectable baby bump.

Grabbing her purse, Annie got out of her car. It was early yet, so parking on Main Street wasn't a problem. The village of Maple Springs waited patiently for the hordes of tourists who'd amble along these sidewalks to shop or grab lunch before returning to the beach across the street.

For now it was quiet and Annie took in the colorful plants and flowers that were stuffed into boxes and gigantic pots adorning store windows and doors. Water drops glimmered in the morning sun. Annie spotted the woman who maintained the downtown's greenery and waved. She waved back while spraying down the hanging flowers anchored to the lampposts.

Maple Springs knew how to capitalize on the short summer season. And Annie appreciated the added dance students this time of year, she really did. But if the truth were told, she preferred the end of the season after the summer folks left and went back to wherever they called home. Until they descended again come winter to ski.

A couple of tinkling bells rang when she opened the door of an old Victorian that served as the historical society's office and museum.

"May I help you— Oh, hello, Annie." The director, Holly, slipped from behind her desk.

"Morning." Annie shook the girl's offered hand and got right to the point. "I'd like to permanently donate some of Jack's collection for an exhibit, but I'll need your help in looking over the considered items."

Holly gave her a broad smile. "Wonderful. I can come by later this week if that works for you."

"Perfect. I'm still working out what to include."

Holly tipped her head. "Is Matthew helping you with that, too? I heard he replaced your roof."

Where'd she hear that? Any why would she ask such a question that was none of her business? "Maybe."

"You know him well, then?" Holly was definitely digging.

"Well enough." Annie considered Holly a moment. Was the woman interested in Matthew? She wouldn't blame her, but really, what was up with the nosy questions? "Do you mind if I look around to get a feel for your displays?"

Holly nodded. "Sure. Go right ahead. I'll get the donation paperwork together. You can grab them on your way out."

"Thanks." Annie's sandals scuffed the hardwood floors as she walked through to the museum rooms. The upstairs was roped off with a sign that stated offices resided there.

Viewing the displays, she felt a stab of sympathy for

Holly. According to Jack, Matthew dated but didn't commit because of his schedule on the lakes. Annie couldn't recall one woman Matthew had talked about or even mentioned other than a passing reference.

Yet another reason to ignore the attraction between them. Annie didn't want to lose Matthew by allowing anything more than friendship to creep between them. Friendship might be the only logical thing they'd share for the long haul.

After looking over one of the permanent exhibits of regional Native American art, Annie wandered back to the office. She picked up the paperwork labeled with her name and promised to call and confirm a time and day for Holly to view Jack's collection and then left.

Pulling out her phone, Annie hit Matthew's name on her screen. He answered right away. "Hi, Matthew? I need to ask you a favor."

"What's that?" She could hear the smile in his voice.

She hesitated a moment. He'd offered to go through Jack's stuff and she welcomed his insight. "I need to decide what to donate to the historical society and wondered if your offer still stands."

"Of course it does. Name the day, and I'll be there."

Annie swallowed a wave of nervousness. "I'm thinking tomorrow night. Do you mind if I have Ginger over, too? I'd like to box up the rest of Jack's clothes while we're at it."

"No problem. What about that oak desk? Does that need to come out or will it stay?"

She laughed. "That was another favor, but there's no hurry. If you want it, you can have it for the price of moving it out."

"My father would love it."

"Then it's yours. But you're going to need more than me to lift it."

"I wouldn't let you lift it even if you could. I'll see if I can bring one of my brothers with me."

"That'd be great. I'll order pizza."

Matthew laughed. "Now you're talking my language."

Annie smiled, relieved. They wouldn't be alone. Even if Ginger couldn't make it. "Thanks, Matthew."

"You're welcome, Annie." His voice softened. "I'm glad you called. If you need anything, remember I'm a phone call away."

"I know." She needed too much. Maybe more than he could ever give.

"Good. I'll see you tomorrow."

"Yup."

After she hung up, she called Ginger. "If you're not busy tomorrow evening, would you like to come over and help me and Matthew clear out Jack's room? No worries if you can't."

"Ah, you're not trying to set me up again, are you?"

Annie laughed. "Of course not. It's just, well…I need his help and don't think it's a good idea to be alone, you know?"

Ginger's voice lowered. "Did something happen between you two?"

Annie hesitated. A kiss had happened. Even though it had happened over two months ago, that kiss had changed things between them. She chose her mother-in-law's rationale instead of the truth. "I'm a widow now and have to consider how things look."

"Annie, what's going on?" Ginger didn't buy it.

"Nothing."

Yet.

Annie ignored that slippery thought. She hadn't misinterpreted the vibe from Matthew the other night or her immediate response. Either way, an ounce of prevention was worth a pound of cure.

"Okay, count me in."

"Good. He might bring his brother along, too, so you never know…"

Ginger laughed. "Nice try. I don't have the time or inclination to date, but don't worry, I'll be there."

"Thanks. I really appreciate it. See you tomorrow."

Pulling her notebook out of her purse, Annie crossed off another to-do item on her list. The two things she'd rather have ignored were now done. Almost.

When she performed with a dance troupe, she knew the show always went on. Annie needed to go on, too. For her baby's sake, she'd get Jack's room emptied out so she could make it into a nursery. For Jack's sake, she'd share his maritime collection with a community that had embraced them when they'd moved here.

And for Matthew's sake, Annie would do what she could to protect their friendship whether they liked it or not.

"So, who is this woman?" Matthew's brother Darren got out of his green work truck with the distinctive Department of Natural Resources logo on the doors.

He was the only brother around without plans for the evening. Matthew had had his work cut out convincing Darren to come, but his brother had finally agreed on the condition that he drove his own vehicle in case he needed to leave early. Some excuse about being on call as backup, but Matthew knew better.

"She's Jack Marshall's wife." Standing in Annie's driveway, Matthew made the correction. "I mean widow."

Darren's eyes softened. "Oh. Man, that's a tough one.

I liked Jack." Then he kicked at Matthew's back tire. "All I need do is move the desk, right? We're not taking it anywhere in town."

"Right." Matthew slapped his brother's back. Darren didn't go into Maple Springs anymore. "Don't worry, man. There's no way you'll run into her."

Darren gave him a sharp look.

Matthew spread his hands. "Am I supposed to ignore the obvious?"

"No. Just don't remind me," his brother growled. Darren's ex-fiancée lived in Maple Springs with a guy who used to be Darren's best friend.

"Thanks for doing this. The desk is big and heavy and in this heat, we might want to consider a jump in the lake after," he continued to tease.

Darren looked around like a man hiding from the mob. "You go ahead, I'm out."

Matthew spotted Annie stepping out onto the porch and his teasing stopped. His jaw may have dropped a little and his pulse certainly picked up speed. She looked cool and so feminine with her hair up and a long and breezy cotton dress swirling around her ankles.

"I'm getting ready to order the pizza, any requests?"

"Pepperoni." Matthew couldn't keep his eyes off her.

"And your brother?" She smiled.

Darren smiled back. "Pepperoni is fine."

Matthew tamped down the sudden urge to wipe that broad grin off his brother's face. "Darren, this is Annie Marshall."

Annie extended her free hand. "Good to meet you. And thank you for your help. Come in, please."

They stepped inside where boxes littered the floor. Ginger struggled with one so Matthew reached out to lend a hand. "I got it, where do you want it?"

"Front porch is fine for now, then they're heading for my car."

Matthew nodded. "Ginger, this is my brother Darren."

Ginger held out a hand and Darren gave her the briefest handshake he'd ever seen. Matthew chuckled as he set the box on the porch. His brother was afraid of the female population as a whole.

While Ginger drilled Darren about the recent closure of a nearby public boat launch for repairs, Matthew followed Annie into the kitchen. "He's in for an earful."

Annie shrugged. "She's worried about anything that might deter tourists from coming into downtown Maple Springs."

"Classic merchant reaction."

"Summer makes or breaks her." Annie reached for glasses from the cupboard.

Matthew didn't know what it was like to depend on the fickle shopping habits of summer residents and tourists for one's income. He supposed he'd be hyper-vigilant too if he were in Ginger's shoes. "So, what's with the boxes?"

Annie poured lemonade over ice and her hand shook a little. "Jack's clothes. Ginger's taking them to the church rummage sale."

"All of them?"

She looked at him. "Most everything. What am I supposed to do with them? I have to get the room cleared in time to make it into a nursery."

He'd never considered the fate of Jack's clothes or how difficult it would be to decide what to keep and what to give away. Or throw away. It'd been tough enough going through Jack's cabin on their freighter. There wasn't much, but Matthew had boxed the items up and dropped them off here. Annie hadn't been home at the time, so he'd given the contents to her aunt from Arizona.

There'd been a framed picture of Jack and Annie when they'd painted this house. Matthew had taken that picture and Jack had kept it on his bedside table in his captain's quarters. In it, Annie had a paint smudge on her cheek and a smile wider than the sky. It was the kind of smile that defined happiness from the inside out like sunshine breaking through a cloud.

One day she'd smile like that again.

Maybe even for him.

He shouldn't go there.

In fact, he shouldn't be here, standing so close. "I'm going to grab that desk with Darren while we wait for the pizza delivery. Might as well get the hard task done and out of the way."

"Right." Annie laughed.

When it came to difficulty, moving Jack's desk was nothing more than physical strength. It was the other stuff that was hard to go through. The things that represented Jack's life and his passions. Even his clothes, simple and classic in style, spelled out who he'd been. An oak desk was nothing compared to those things.

He stilled Annie's hands as she quickly loaded a tray with glasses of ice and a pitcher of lemonade and napkins. "Annie, you can slow down. You don't have to get rid of everything all at once."

She gripped his hands hard before letting go. "Jack wouldn't want me to keep shrines. He'd want me to move forward, not stay stuck."

Matthew nodded in agreement. Jack was not a look-back-with-regret kind of guy. Always forward, always improving, he'd inspired Matthew to be a better deck officer, even a better man. Maybe that's why Jack had a fascination with maritime history. He liked to measure how far they'd come and how far it was possible to go.

"Thanks for the desk."

"You're welcome." Annie lifted the tray and headed for the living room.

Matthew followed her. Could her moving on include him? For the first time in his life, Matthew hoped for more then he'd ever thought he wanted. A future with a woman. And that woman was Annie Marshall.

"That's the last of it." Annie stood on the grass near the driveway. They'd loaded boxes for the church rummage sale into the back of Ginger's car.

Ginger glanced from her to Matthew and then back to her. "Talk to you tomorrow?"

"Sure." Annie hugged her friend. "Thank you for everything."

Ginger squeezed tight and the let go. "Of course. Anytime."

She watched her friend slip into her car and back out. Darren had left only moments before, and Matthew hadn't made any move to leave yet even though they were done with Jack's collection.

It hadn't taken long to decide which items she'd donate to the historical society. Matthew had chosen well and even his brother and Ginger had agreed that the compilation of stuff was interesting and would make a fine exhibit for Maple Springs.

Jack would be honored to be so remembered.

Annie waved as her friend drove away and then brushed her hands against her belly. Facing her house, she hesitated. She couldn't invite Matthew inside and yet she didn't want to go back in there alone.

Despite going through Jack's things, she'd enjoyed having company and laughing like a normal person with friends.

Matthew stood next to her. "You want to go for a walk?"

Had he sensed her reluctance? "I'll just grab my purse and lock the door."

"I'll be right here." Matthew sat down on the top porch step and waited.

Annie entered to the quiet, empty feeling that remained after company left. That stillness was usually a welcome thing, but tonight it suffocated her. Most of Jack's things would soon be gone along with his clothes. She'd saved special items she'd never part with, but it was as if she'd swept him out of the house. Gone, but never forgotten.

Jack...

Her husband's absence screamed louder with his clothes gone and much of his stuff sorted into *keep* and *go* piles. Those piles were a billboard announcement that Jack wasn't ever coming back.

Closure.

It's what the pastor had predicted she'd find. What about being comfortable alone? Single. When would that happen?

Slipping through to the kitchen, Annie grabbed her wallet and keys and threw them in a smaller purse, one she could easily loop over her head. Exiting the front door she locked up behind her.

"I thought we'd get some ice cream."

Annie smiled. "That'd be great."

He offered his hand.

She took it without hesitation. They walked the couple of blocks to town in comfortable silence. She needed this. She needed the quiet comfort of simply holding his hand. How did he know? Did he feel that same letting go of Jack as she?

Rallying her courage she asked, "What are you thinking?"

"I'm trying not to."

She laughed. Maybe it was better not to examine whatever it was between them. Especially the warmth of their entwined fingers. "I know what you mean."

He looked at her. "You did well going through Jack's maritime collection. I know it wasn't easy."

It hadn't been easy for him, either. They'd reminisced about when and where Jack had found each item since Matthew had been on several of those outings. "I couldn't have done it without your help. Thanks."

He squeezed her hand. "You're welcome."

They wound their way toward the waterfront and the small ice cream stand that stayed open late during the summer months. The evening sun hung low in the western sky like an orange beach ball. No clouds marred its hazy light, and the fuzzy reflection on the stillness of Maple Bay was broken only by kids who swam at the public beach. Their adolescent squeals, as they splashed and jumped off the dock, pierced the humid night air.

Stepping into line for ice cream, Annie heard her name called, and turned. One of her young dance students walked toward them between her parents. Her student's mom gave Matthew a curious glance.

Annie let go of his hand. "Hi, Belinda. Here for ice cream?"

"Best in town." Belinda's gaze narrowed. "I am so sorry to hear about your husband's death. How are you?"

Annie's face tightened. "I'm fine, all things considered."

Belinda's gaze raked over Matthew once again. "Yes, yes, I imagine so. Well, good to see you. I think we'll wait for the line to go down before ordering. Come on, Paisley."

Annie watched the woman drag her seven-year old away while whispering to the bored-looking man who was her husband.

"Who was that?" Matthew asked.

"A client. Her daughter is in my beginner ballet class."

"Hmmph." He rubbed his chin.

"What?"

Matthew shrugged. "Kind of snobby."

Annie laughed. "Maybe a little, but she gives a lot to the local arts council and—"

He stopped her with a raised hand. "No need to explain, I know the type. I grew up here, remember?"

"That's right. You're a local yokel."

Matthew grinned. "And the reason why there's a lifeguard stationed on that dock until sunset."

"What did you do?"

"Too much horseplay between my brothers and cousins. We owned that dock in the summer and wouldn't let other kids on it. The parks and recreation department finally posted a lifeguard after several complaints and it stuck. They've had one ever since."

Annie laughed. She didn't know a whole lot about his family other than the maple syrup and ice fishing. "How many of you are there?"

"I'm one of ten. Three older brothers, three younger brothers and three younger sisters."

"Wow. That's a huge family."

Matthew shrugged. "Never a dull moment."

"And never alone, if you don't want to be."

He looked at her closely, his eyes sad. "Annie—"

It was their turn in line, so Annie stepped up to the screened window and asked for a small vanilla soft serve.

"With all the freaky things you eat, that's one dull cone." Matthew nudged her with his shoulder before ordering a double scoop of German chocolate-cake-flavored ice cream in a waffle cone.

Annie shook her head. "That sounds like a big bellyache."

He grinned as he took the confection and paid for both. "Not possible."

"Thanks for buying."

"You got the pizza," Matthew mumbled around a mouthful of ice cream.

"The least I could do." Annie nudged him back with her shoulder and smiled.

Matthew steered her toward a park bench overlooking the bay. "Let's catch the sunset."

"Deal." Annie slid onto it while licking the melting streams of ice cream before they hit her hand.

Matthew sat next to her. Right next to her. Then he draped his arm around the back of the bench. His fingers grazed her skin at the top of her shoulder making her shudder.

"Cold?"

"Must be the ice cream."

He wrapped his arm more firmly around her and scooted her against him. "Better?"

She resisted the urge to snuggle into him, and nodded. The warmth and close contact staved off that empty feeling of being alone. All alone.

Annie's glimpse of her future wasn't pretty without Jack.

Matthew gave her a comforting squeeze.

She leaned her head against his shoulder. They finished their ice cream cones and listened to the sounds of kids splashing at the beach. The sun dipped low until it was swallowed up by Lake Michigan.

They didn't speak. They didn't have to. All Annie knew was that she didn't want to go home.

Matthew brushed his lips against her forehead. "You okay?"

She shrugged. "I hate this."

"I know. Jack's death left a hole that will take time to fill. Work's not the same. You're not the same."

Annie pulled back and looked at him. "Time isn't something I'm fond of."

Matthew traced the side of her face with his thumb. "Aww, Annie, I'd take the emptiness away if I could."

Dear, kind Matthew. He understood. Even more so than Ginger. She cupped his face. "I know you would."

He leaned close and touched his lips to hers for the briefest of sweet kisses.

Annie ended it before she kissed him too deeply in return. It wouldn't be fair to give into this misplaced desire to escape from grief. No matter how badly she'd like to forget the pain, she wouldn't use Matthew to do it.

"I better get back home." She needed to deal with her empty house before the sky grew dark and starry.

He stood and took her hand. "Let's go."

When she turned, Annie spotted Holly from the historical society with an ice cream cone in hand and a smug look of satisfaction on her face.

Annie let go of Matthew's hand.

Holly waved while she waited for her friend to catch up, but it was too late run for cover. The two young women walked straight for them.

Holly grinned with barely contained glee. "Steamy night, huh?"

"We're in for a hot summer at this rate," Matthew answered, clueless to the young woman's true meaning.

Annie's stomach dropped to the soles of her flip-flops. Holly Miller had seen their kiss on the bench. The kiss had been brief and comforting, but the triumphant glare in the director's eyes said otherwise. The young woman looked as if she'd stumbled upon a torrid tidbit. And there wasn't much Annie could do or say without making things appear worse.

"I'll stop by your office tomorrow and confirm a time for you to view my donation."

Holly gave a smug nod. "Perfect. I look forward to it."

Annie didn't. Taking a deep breath, she started counting her steps back to the house.

Chapter Eight

June

Annie refunded the remaining fees for her third dance student pulled from summer classes by their moms. Sometimes kids changed their minds after a class or two, but three on the same Monday?

She spotted the bouquet of flowers Matthew had given her well over a week ago and sighed. She loved flowers. Jack hadn't been the kind of guy who gave her flowers. The excuse he'd used was that she grew her own. But then he hadn't bought her candy or jewelry, either. Jack's gifts had always been house-driven and practical.

Matthew's flowers were wilted now. Several petals had fallen off and lay on her desk, circling the vase. Time to throw them away.

She hated to admit it, but she'd missed seeing Matthew this past weekend. He'd gone away with his brothers for a three-day weekend of fishing and camping in Canada. Was it truly about missing the man or the attention he gave her?

She missed Jack. She missed the attention given by a husband to his wife. Even though Annie was used to plenty of alone time while Jack was on the lakes, back then she knew he'd come home. Not now, though. Not ever again. And she craved that sense of belonging that she'd had with Jack. Craved his touch. His love.

Her office phone rang, startling her thoughts. "Hello, Marshall's Movement."

"I'm across the street at the pharmacy and noticed you're still there. Do you want to grab some dinner?" Ginger's voice sounded tight at the other end.

Annie glanced at the clock reading seven-thirty. She hadn't eaten since lunch and felt a little hollow. "That'd be great."

"I'll be over in five minutes."

Annie disconnected and then organized her desk. Her last class had ended an hour ago, and then there'd been the paperwork to do with those three cancelation calls. But it didn't take long before Ginger knocked on the front door.

"Where to?" Annie met her outside and locked up.

"Bernelli's?"

Annie chuckled and agreed.

The trendy coffee-and-sandwich shop had opened a year ago. Ginger, once a hardcore tea drinker, was hooked on their mocha lattés.

"How was your weekend?" Ginger's eyes danced.

"Quiet. I had classes, planted my garden and slept a lot."

Annie had left a message on Matthew's cell, thanking him for tilling the soil of her garden. She hadn't seen his watch, though. She'd purchased seeds and tomato plants, glad that he'd encouraged her to put in a garden this year.

Ginger had been gone, too, attending an herb and spice grower's convention. She looked at her friend. "How was yours? Pick up any mysterious new tea leaves?"

Ginger laughed. "No, but I found a couple new vendors I'd like to try. Even a local gal who grows some organic stuff."

Once they were seated with their orders given, Ginger couldn't seem to sit still. She fiddled with her napkin and looked around the small coffee shop.

"Everything okay?" Something was up. Ginger was a live wire and right now she looked ready to shoot sparks.

"Yeah, sure. Why?"

Annie rolled her eyes while she waited. "Because you can't sit still."

Her friend leaned back and sighed. "Hmm, not sure how to word this."

"Just say it straight out, like ripping off a Band-Aid."

Ginger sipped her iced tea instead, prolonging the agony.

"Gin-gerrr." Annie sat at the edge of her seat.

"Okay, here goes." A deep breath. "I overheard a couple of customers talking about you and Matthew on the beach the other night. I thought you should know."

Annie cocked her head. "We took a walk and got ice cream after you and Darren left. So?"

Ginger bit her bottom lip and looked away, clearly uncomfortable. "So, I heard that you were all over each other."

"What!" Annie's voice rose.

A couple of people at nearby tables looked their way. Quietly, Annie prodded, "Who said so?"

Ginger sipped her tea again. "A couple of women from Bay Willows were talking. I don't know who they were. They paid in cash but referenced you by name. That's what piqued my interest."

Annie had several seasonal dance students from the nearby summer community of Bay Willows. An image of Holly Miller's smug face flashed before her eyes. But Holly had been nothing less than polite and professional when she'd viewed the collection of Jack's things for donation.

Why would she spread such ugly gossip? Was it someone else, like Paisley's mom? Belinda had been one of the mothers who'd pulled their daughters from class for the summer.

Annie grasped her neck and her skin felt hot. "What exactly did they say?"

"I only heard the tail end about 'that dance instructor all over a younger man.'" Ginger leaned close, eyes wide. "Maybe this is none of my business, but what's going on with you two?"

Annie rubbed her temples. That barb about a younger man stung. Was their age difference that obvious? Holly knew Matthew's age. She'd gone to school with him. "It's my fault."

Ginger's eyes grew big and round. "What is?"

She felt the heat crawl from her neck to her face, burning her cheeks. "We held hands, but we were not *all over each other.* Although, we kissed, but it was only a peck, a comfort thing. Nothing to get all worked up over."

And a far cry from the kiss they'd shared after the funeral. What if she told Ginger about that? Her friend would no doubt be horrified, and rightly so.

Ginger grabbed her hand. "It's okay, Annie."

"Is it? What if I'm transferring my feelings for Jack, missing him the way I do, onto Matthew's shoulders?"

Ginger gave her a goofy grin. "But what a pair of shoulders, huh?"

Annie laughed. It came out sounding a little hysterical, but that was better than sobbing. "I don't want to use him. What if I'm using him as a shield against my grief?"

She squeezed her hand before letting go as their sandwich orders had arrived. "You've known each other a long time. What if there's real love growing out of your shared grief? Who's to say how long is too long or not long enough to find that out?"

Annie didn't buy it. Always the optimist, Ginger looked at the best in every situation. But Annie wasn't sure there was one here. She deeply loved her dead husband. Still and always.

Till death do us part...

Jack was gone. It might be okay to find love again, down the road, but she couldn't love Matthew. Not this soon. And that's what made it so awful. And the subject of town gossip.

She'd always cared about Matthew on a friendly level, but this attraction was new territory. It was scary how easy he was to lean on. Couple that with her fears about having a baby by herself, and bam, Matthew had become her hero with his promise to help. He'd stepped into Jack's role and she let him. Encouraged him, even. How selfish could she be?

Ginger grabbed her hand again. "Annie, please don't freak over this. I only wanted to give you a heads-up. Let's pray, okay?"

Annie nodded, not trusting her voice. She should pray more often, but her confidence in God had been shaken. Prayer was the answer to life's questions, fears and doubts. But then, trust in her judgment wasn't exactly at a high place, either.

What did she really know? Nothing felt secure anymore.

Her thoughts wandered as Ginger prayed over the food and for her and her baby. Annie remembered Matthew's simple prayer of thanks, the Zelinsky dinnertime prayer.

Bless us, oh Lord, and these Thy gifts...

It hit her then. She'd lost three dance students due to gossip. Gossip fueled by her own careless actions. If she wasn't careful, she might lose everything.

"What's got you smiling?" Darren drove while Luke played a game on his phone and their other brother Cam snoozed in the backseat.

Matthew had listened to his voice mail as soon as they were through the Sault Ste. Marie border crossing and heading south on I-75 back in Michigan. Customs hadn't been bad for the first Tuesday in June when tourists were usually crawling all over to visit the Soo Locks. But, then, it was still morning.

"Annie planted her garden this past weekend." She'd called last night and left the message.

Darren looked amused. "And that's a big deal, why?"

He wasn't at liberty to explain why that good news made him smile. Annie's energy was coming back, proving the morning sickness and exhaustion had lessened. Was she home free to carry the baby to term?

"He's got a thing for her," Luke added.

"That's obvious."

Matthew looked sharp. "How so?"

Darren laughed. "The other night you were all over her."

He wasn't, either. "What are you talking about?"

"If you weren't touching her hand or back or helping her carry something, you kept looking at her."

Matthew shrugged. "So?"

"So nothing. She's a beautiful woman. I get it."

The urge to defend his reactions scratched like sandpaper. It was way more than Annie's looks Matthew appreciated. "Yeah."

Darren chuckled again.

"What?"

"I've never seen you serious about anyone before."

Matthew didn't answer right away. He'd made some serious promises, but those were about the baby. He stared at the interstate ahead. They were about two hours or so from home. And Annie and her garden. He'd never looked forward to seeing someone as he did her.

"She's a good friend," Matthew finally said.

Darren didn't look convinced. "Uh-huh. Have you introduced her to Mom and Dad?"

"They met her once before when Annie came out and picked up Jack from ice fishing. Oh, and then again at the funeral."

"Wow, Matty, that was only three months ago."

He nodded. Seemed longer, and yet finding Jack dead in his cabin felt more recent, like yesterday. It might be too early to do anything about these *serious* feelings.

"Man, I hope this works out for you." Darren looked grim. But then he was a man scorned by love and that kind of hurt had twisted him. He was a lot gloomier than he used to be.

"Yeah, me, too." What else could he say?

Later that afternoon, Matthew stood on Annie's front porch with a small bouquet of locally grown flowers that he'd picked up at the IGA. The store had a couple buckets of them for five dollars, so he figured, why not? Annie loved flowers.

He knocked on her door.

She opened it, her eyes wide. "Matthew."

"Hey." He handed her the flowers. "These are for you."

"I love peonies." She buried her nose in the pink ones with the strongest scent. Then she stepped out onto the porch, closing the door behind her. "Thank you. These are beautiful."

So was she.

She hadn't changed from her work. She wore a fitted T-shirt brandishing her studio logo and billowy pants. "Don't you want to put them in water?"

She hesitated. "I will."

He cocked his head. What was wrong with her? A streak of something dark and unfamiliar seared his gut. "Is somebody here?"

"No."

Relief hit him hard. "Are you going to invite me in or what?"

"Why are you here?" She still hadn't moved.

"I thought I'd stop by and see how you did on your garden."

"Oh, okay, come on." She walked off the porch and headed for the backyard.

Matthew stayed put a minute before following her. Catching up, he stalled her with a touch of his hand. "Annie, what's going on?"

"What do you mean?"

"Don't play dumb. I've been over hundreds of times and now you won't let me in. How come?"

She rubbed her forehead and looked around. "Not here."

He looked around, too. "What?"

She grabbed his hand and pulled him into the back-yard, then let go as she made her way up the steps of her back deck. She swapped his flowers out with a drooping branch of lilacs in a vase on the table. "Thanks for these."

He took the steps until he stood near her. Placing his hands on her shoulders he turned her to face him. "I saw them and thought of you. What's going on?"

She let out a deep sigh. "I lost three dance students yesterday. Their moms pulled them out and asked for refunds…"

"Yeah?" he coaxed. "What does that have to do—"

She stepped back from him and sat down. "There's gossip going around about the two of us, and I think those kids were pulled because of it. Because of that night we got ice cream."

He sat across from her, hoping she hadn't lost a marble or two while he was gone. "What happened the night we got ice cream?"

"Seriously?" Now she looked hurt. "You don't remember that you kissed me—"

"That was barely even a kiss." Matthew let out a nervous laugh. "That's all you're worried about?"

Now she looked angry. "No. I'm worried about my reputation. My livelihood depends on it."

"And you think your dance students left because of a little kiss?"

"They were pulled because I'm newly widowed and running wild with a younger man."

He narrowed his gaze. Annie's behavior could hardly be called *wild*. The kiss they'd shared after the funeral, though… "Is that what you think you're doing?"

She stared him down pretty hard. "I don't know, maybe."

"Annie—"

"I lost three paid clients because of whatever *this is* between us. It's leaking out for all to see."

Matthew wanted to tell her it shouldn't matter what other people thought or said about them. Especially the shallow folks who'd spread such venom. But considering her position, he paused before voicing those thoughts.

As Darren had said, it had only been three months.

He sighed, feeling like he'd swallowed a lead buoy. "So what do you want to do?"

She shrugged and looked away.

He took both her hands in his. "I'm not leaving a friend in need high and dry because of a few rumors."

"Is that what we are? Friends." Her eyes filled with tears and her voice sounded raw.

She'd lost Jack. No way was he walking away from her, too. He wanted to pull her into his arms but reached for her hand instead. "No, Annie, we're more than just friends. And I want more still, but you have to want that, too. Until you do, I'll wait it out."

A tear spilled over the rim of her eye to trail down her cheek. She sniffed. "No more kisses, okay?"

That was a tall order he wasn't sure he could abide. Especially now. "You mean in public?"

Ignoring his attempt to tease, she lifted their joined hands. "And *this* has got to stop. Especially in public."

He groaned. "Now you're killing me."

"Be serious." But she chuckled, too. "I'm too old for you."

Whatever she'd heard, the difference in their ages had been the one that stung most. He grew serious in an instant. "No, you're not, Annie. Not in my eyes. You're beautiful."

Her eyes grew all watery again. "Ugh, hormones. I'm so emotional." She pulled her hands away and scrubbed her eyes with both palms.

Matthew stood. He needed to rethink his plans for the rest of the day. He'd hoped they could hang out together, but now? Maybe that wasn't such a good idea. "Show me this garden of yours and then I'll be on my way."

She trotted down the steps and spread her arms wide.

"Here it is. I even put in eggplant. I had the room thanks to you, but I'm sorry about your watch."

"No problem. I got another one." He lifted his arm to show her.

"Nice." She hardly gave it a glance.

"I think so."

Taking in the sight of newly mounded dirt and tiny tomato plants in neat little rows, he tamped down his anger. Annie had enough to deal with. She didn't need pettiness from some of Maple Springs's *finest* bringing her down, too.

So, he'd keep a friendly distance for now, but he'd find out who started that gossip. He might not be able to put a stop to it, but he'd find out who stirred the pot. Starting with a certain director of the historical society.

That had gone better than she'd expected. Annie glanced at Matthew's rigid stance while he looked over her garden and breathed a little easier. She wasn't sure how he'd react and wouldn't have blamed him if he'd simply left.

Hadn't she heard him tell Jack that he hated all the drama that came with a relationship? Well, she was giving Matthew all that and then some. Yet he not only remained, he wanted more. He wanted her.

She rubbed her stomach to quell a sudden flip—no, it was more like what she imagined moths dancing around a porch light might feel like. *The baby?*

"You okay?" Matthew looked at her, curious.

"Fine." She wanted to keep this incredible sensation to herself. It might be nothing. And she wasn't about to let Matthew touch her midsection. He wouldn't feel anything, anyway. The movement had been deep inside her belly.

He narrowed his gaze.

"What?"

"You look, ah, fuller." He grinned.

She flushed and looked down at her feet in the grass. Her clothes either didn't fit or fit more snugly than they used to. Especially her tops. Not a bad thing to finally have some womanly curves.

"When's your next doctor's appointment?" He hadn't forgotten.

Maybe she shouldn't let him go with her considering the gossip, but what if she received bad news? Having him with her for support took on new importance and even urgency. He seemed to know what she needed, completely in tune. She needed him there. How was that wrong?

"Next week."

"I'd still like to go."

Annie nodded. "I'd like that."

He reached out to touch her, but pushed her hair back instead. "Don't worry, okay?"

Easier said than done, but she agreed. "Okay."

"Well, I guess I better go." He let out a deep breath and then leaned close and whispered, "In case anyone's lurking in the shadows, spying on us."

She pushed at him. "It's not funny."

"I know, but it's not the end of the world, either. Come on, walk me to my truck."

Annie agreed that was probably true. If only she could get a handle on her emotions and ignore the urge to embrace Matthew every time she saw him.

But she wanted to be held—for comfort and not for comfort. Knowing he was truly interested in her as a woman, not only an obligation to Jack, zipped through her like a spring rain that washed away crusty old snow.

"Hey, what are you doing the rest of the day?" Matthew asked.

Annie stopped walking. "Not much. Why?"

"Let's go somewhere."

She thought about that. "Where?"

"Mackinac City? The Island. Anywhere you want."

Over thirty miles away from Maple Springs, away from everything and everyone, sounded good. Really good. She glanced at her empty house. She didn't want to spend another evening home alone. As long as they didn't hang out in town, what harm could there be?

"Are you in the mood to ride bikes around Mackinac Island?"

His gaze lingered on her middle. "You can do that?"

"Of course I can. It's been years since I was there."

Matthew grinned. "Let's go."

Annie smiled back. "Let me change real quick, what about you?"

Matthew wore shorts and a T-shirt. "I'm ready."

She laughed, feeling young. Spontaneous. Free. Normal. "I'll be right back."

Annie wasn't going to let gossip stop her. They'd be far away from anyone who might care. It might be late afternoon, but they had all evening to enjoy. This early in June the last ferry back from Mackinac Island wasn't until eight or nine so she'd be home before dark.

They had all evening.

Chapter Nine

"The lilacs will be in full bloom." Annie grabbed her ball cap before it blew off her head. The passenger ferry they rode revved to top speed.

Water sprayed like fine mist when they bounced on a wave. It felt good considering the heat of the day. Only the beginning of June and yet they'd had a hot start of summerlike weather.

"Yeah." Matthew brushed droplets of water from his knees.

His mother had lilac bushes. They grew well all over northern Michigan, ambling wild along the road and in fields. Something about the sandy soil made them flourish. Mackinac Island celebrated peak bloom time with a festival that happened to be the upcoming weekend. They'd certainly see lilacs.

He and Annie sat on the open top deck of a newer boat that belonged to one of three Mackinac Island ferry companies. The thing hauled. It wasn't exactly packed as not many headed to the island this late on a Tuesday afternoon. Seating was scattered with mainly young people enjoying the twenty-minute ride.

"Lilacs remind me of my mother," Annie said.

"Your parents aren't alive." Matthew remembered Jack telling him that once. In fact, this was the first time he'd ever heard Annie mention them.

"Killed in a car accident when I was in college. I got the call from my aunt right before a big audition."

"What happened?"

Annie grinned at him. "I landed one of the leads."

She had powered through the pain even then. Or maybe, that's when she'd learned how. "Did anyone know about the accident?"

"No. I didn't want them to. And that might have been one of my best performances."

Matthew wished he had gone to see her dance. Jack used to brag that Annie had been something special up on stage, and Matthew imagined that to be true. She certainly moved with grace and lightness at her studio. Annie might be lithe and lean, but she was also strong. She had to be to hold those positions as long as she did.

Annie Marshall was stronger than she realized.

"I forgot how gorgeous this is." Annie looked around, soaking in the sight of the mighty Mackinac Bridge. "The last time I went to Mackinac Island was after Jack and I moved to Maple Springs. That was almost five years ago. Sad, I haven't been back since. Thank you for suggesting this."

Matthew nodded. He was glad he'd thought of it. He didn't want her powering through the pain of losing Jack alone. Annie needed a fun time away from home. He was beginning to think he might need her. Annie Marshall was the kind of woman he'd always wanted but had never found.

He glanced at her hands. Her wedding ring sparkled in the sunshine. What would Jack think about all this?

Matthew had always cared for Annie, maybe too

much. He searched the expanse of dark blue water that met a lighter blue, clear and cloudless sky. A perfect day. He'd do his best to keep it that way by maintaining a friendly distance.

He spotted an oceangoing boat heading through the Straits and slipping under the Mackinac Bridge. He pointed. "There's a salty."

Annie leaned forward, shielding her eyes from the sun. "Can you tell where it's from?"

He shrugged. "Netherlands, maybe?"

"Cool." She looked up at him. "Are you anxious to get back on the lakes?"

For once, he wasn't. "Not in a big hurry, no."

She smiled.

He smiled back. And wanted to throw everything about maintaining friendship overboard. Annie worried too much about gossip.

When the red-and-white lighthouse came into view as they turned toward the island's harbor, Matthew worried over their plan yet again. "Do you think it's a good idea to ride bikes?"

"Why wouldn't it be?"

It was less than ten miles around Mackinac Island staying on the paved shoreline path. The rental bikes were for touring with fat seats and baskets. There were gentle sloping hills along the shore, but still. "What if you fall?"

Annie patted his knee. Her wedding ring winked at him again, warning him that her heart was still Jack's. "I won't fall. I can still ride a bike, you know. Exercise is a good thing, and happens to be my occupation. And my doctor agrees. An easy bike ride isn't something strenuous. I'll be careful. We'll take it slow."

"No Tour-de-France speeds." He took her hand and held it.

"We have to take a lot of things slow."

"Right."

"We could rent a horse-drawn carriage instead."

Considering that nothing but bicycles and horses were allowed as transportation, they'd definitely keep a leisurely pace. But then sitting side by side in a buggy built for two invited romance, and they were here to have fun—the friendly kind of fun.

Annie scrunched her nose. "Bikes are cheaper and easier to stop if we want to explore the shoreline. I wore my bathing suit just in case."

Matthew chuckled. Annie had not only demanded to pay her own way, she'd come prepared. A couple of beach towels were also stuffed in her backpack.

Another thought plagued him. "Water's going to be cold yet. Will that be okay?"

She pinched his hand and then let go. "And you're the one telling me not to worry. I'll be fine. I've been reading what I can and can't do as the pregnancy progresses. Trust me, my doctor okayed swimming, too."

He glanced at Annie's feet. She wore the same brand of sporty sandals that can be worn in the water as he. A good thing considering the shore was pretty much pebbles and rocks.

The ferry put into dock with a shudder of reverse engines. The deck hands tied up and then the green light was given to exit. The dash began and Matthew followed Annie down the stairs and off the boat.

The long wooden dock leading to the main street was a fury of activity. People stood in line with their Mackinac Island trinkets and ice cream cones waiting to catch the next ferry back to the mainland. Hotel personnel loaded luggage and supplies onto horse-drawn carts.

Kids darted, parents corralled and the sun blazed overhead. He heard his name called and looked around.

"Hey, Zelinsky!" One of his wheelsmen that lived on the eastern side of the state waved and walked toward them.

He laughed. "They let you off the *Block*? What are you doing here?"

"Doing the tourist thing with the family. They're supposed to meet me right here, but they're late. What about you?"

Matthew turned toward Annie. "Jimmy, this is Annie Marshall."

Jimmy's eyes widened as he recognized her and offered his hand. "Mrs. Marshall. How are you? We sure miss Jack. The *William Lee Block* ain't the same without him, but then this guy probably already told you that."

Annie shook it with vigor, smiling. "Yes, thanks, and I'm okay."

"Hanging out with this goofball, huh?" Jimmy didn't look shocked, or even surprised.

"Umm, yeah." She let out a nervous-sounding laugh.

Jimmy looked at him, then Annie, then back to him and smiled. "Good. Good for you. Well, there's the family, gotta run."

Matthew watched the guy walk away. "See? No big deal. Guys don't care if we're together."

Annie's brow furrowed. Maybe she didn't believe him. "Some might."

After they'd rented two bikes with complimentary water bottles, they trekked away from the hubbub of town with the plan to grab dinner and hit the shops later, after their ride. Passing by the main park filled with clumps of huge lilac bushes in bloom, Annie scanned the deep lavenders and purples of bursting flowers.

Their sweet scent teased her nose, but instead of pulling over to inhale, she kept pedaling. And fretted over Jimmy's assumption that she and Matthew were together. She'd once heard that men could be worse gossips than women. If so, it'd be all over Jack's freighter that they were seeing each other.

And they were. They were on Mackinac Island like any dating couple. Would the crew think less of her because of it?

She sighed.

"Hey, let's stop here a minute." Matthew had been riding behind her until the bike traffic had thinned but had come up alongside of her.

"So soon?" They hadn't gone much more than a mile, but she pulled over as asked and gently laid her bike down, not trusting the kickstand off-pavement.

Matthew held out his hand. "Come on, I have an idea."

She took it and they ambled closer to the water. This seemed an odd place for a swim. "Should I grab the towels?"

"No." Matthew looked around and then pointed at a little outcropping of rocks. "There. That's the spot. Come on."

"Spot for what?"

He looked at her then. "I think we should build a rock cairn in Jack's memory. And we should build it together."

Annie felt her throat tighten. There were many of the little rock structures already dotting the shoreline. "Nice."

"I think so." He let go of her and searched the immediate area until he found a couple large and sort of flat, smooth rocks for their base.

She made a pile of various sizes and then sat down. Silently, they started placing rocks on top of each other. Larger to smaller, they stacked carefully. And with each rock, Annie felt a sense of letting go.

She glanced at Matthew.

His handsome face looked serious as he touched the rocks with reverence. He looked up and caught her watching him and gave her a shadow of a smile.

Words weren't needed. She didn't want to talk, anyway. She might admit to the odd notion that this was some kind of guilt offering for the growing attraction between them. And like those inadequate sacrifices noted in the Old Testament, stacking a few rocks wouldn't make them clean.

She couldn't shake that imaginary scarlet letter sewn into her heart even though she hadn't done anything wrong. *Not yet.*

Dear Lord, please...

That seemed like the only prayer she could say lately. Closing her eyes, she asked God to delve into her heart and help her figure out that tangled mess.

When they finally finished, they sat silent on the rocky beach next to their rock monument and stared out over Lake Huron. Annie spotted a freighter in the distance. One of the big bulk freighters like the *William Lee Block*, the one Jack had captained. A fitting sight and oddly comforting, too.

She pointed toward it, but Matthew was already watching its slow slice through the water. "Would you look at that?"

"Heading up the St. Mary's." Matthew's hair looked windblown from the ferry ride over. The sun-lightened ends of his sandy brown hair curled in crazy directions and the tanned skin of his face was rough with stubble along his jaw. He made one handsome sailor.

She stood. "Ready to go?"

"Ah, yeah." Matthew stood, too. He used his phone to take a picture of their rock cairn.

Annie grabbed hers and did the same. "Good idea."

He gripped her waist as they walked toward the bikes. "Watch your step."

"I can walk." She pushed away. "What is going on with you?"

"I don't know." He stopped and faced her, running his hands through his hair. "I feel responsible for you now that there's a baby. I don't know, but it's like if I'm not on my game and something happens—"

He looked off toward that freighter and then blew out his breath. "I can't let Jack down again. He'd want me to protect his kid. And you."

Annie's heart broke at the haunted look in his eyes. "Matthew…"

He held up his hand. "Don't."

She remained quiet. He was mourning, too. Trying to deal the best way he could, and part of that had to do with her. He'd said he wanted more. Well, maybe she did, too. Was that so bad?

After a few moments, she smiled. "No more somber sadness, okay? Not today. We're here to have fun."

He looked grim but nodded. "And fun we will have."

"Good." Annie reached her bike and climbed on, but took a swig from her water bottle before pedaling back onto the two-lane asphalt path.

She understood his position. His reasoning, even. They were friends because of Jack. They were probably drawn to each other because of their connection to Jack. Annie didn't want Matthew to be a replacement for the dead husband she missed. Annie would always miss Jack. She cared for Matthew, she really did, but was she falling for him?

If she was, she wanted it to be because of who he was, not because she needed someone to fill the void. So far, Matthew had been the one giving so much support while she received. It was her turn to give back and that meant testing the waters of this relationship a little.

By the time they'd made it over halfway around the island, Annie was hot and sweaty. She didn't care how cold the water was, she needed to cool down. "I'm about ready for a swim. How 'bout you?"

"Yeah."

She spotted a freight-shipping dock where a few kids were jumping in and climbing out by ladder. The water was aquamarine blue and then deeper blue beyond. Gorgeous. "What about here?"

Matthew shook his head. "I'd rather you wade in than jump. Come on. There's a nice beach expanse up ahead."

Annie looked at the inviting water. There was a spot to wade in, but not much of a beach area. She shouldn't chance jumping off that docking ledge, anyway. "Okay, you take the lead."

Matthew rode ahead of her. It wasn't far until he pulled over at a busy fork in the path. On the left, folks lined up at a concession stand and nearby restrooms. There was also a trail that led inland. On the right lay a huge expanse of pebbled beach with an awesome view of the Mackinac Bridge stretched over the deep blue waters of the Straits. Next to the path sat an ancient cannon perched seemingly ready for action.

British Landing.

Holding on to her bike, she read the historical marker

about an amphibious landing by the British in 1812. She felt Matthew standing close beside her. He leaned forward to read the sign and his arm brushed hers, causing her stomach to flip.

"I never realized the British had come here." Her voice sounded tight.

"Hmm. Want something else to drink? Or an ice cream?"

She glanced at the busy stand. "No way. That's too big a line. We've still got water. Let's swim first."

He looked hesitant, as if he didn't quite believe that swimming was a good idea for her. But then he nodded. "We can leave the bikes against that tree over there. Come on."

She followed him.

Matthew grabbed her backpack from his basket. "Let's walk down the beach to where it's less crowded."

She took his hand, knowing he offered it to keep her steady on the rocky beach more than anything else. The rocks were neither big nor craggy, making it easy enough for even little kids to run around near the shore. She was perfectly capable of making her way, but she'd let him do the protective thing. For his sake more than hers, but then she gladly held on, too.

They walked the shoreline away from the crowd when Matthew stopped. "How's this?"

"Perfect."

She helped spread out their towels and looked around. No one she recognized or knew in sight. Not that she expected to see anyone from town. Mackinac Island was loaded with tourists this time of year and today was no exception. Plenty of those tourists waded in the rounded bay. And no one paid them a bit of attention.

Matthew stripped off his T-shirt. "Let's do this."

Annie felt her eyes widen at the sight of his broad chest. Nerves and anticipation jumbled at once, making her feel like an unsure teenager on her first date. "I can walk into the water by myself. I'm not eighty, you know."

He winked at her. "But you're half that, right?"

She bent down for a smooth pebble and tossed it at him.

"Hey." He laughed and ran straight into the water and dove under. He came back up with a roar of delight. "It's cold, but feels good!"

Annie wasn't the *run-right-in* kind of girl. She took her time. Slipping off her shorts, ball cap and T-shirt, she carefully waded in, shaking her hands as she went. "Brrr. It's freezing!"

It wasn't really. Her feet and calves got used to the cool water real quick. And it did feel great, warmed early from the hot spring they'd had.

Matthew came toward her wearing a worried look.

She shooed him back. "I'm kidding, it's fine. I'll be fine. It just takes me a while to get in."

"I'm not waiting all day." He splashed her.

"Cut it out."

He did it again, and then ran forward and scooped her up.

She squealed, but held on. "Matthew, don't."

But he was already taking her toward deeper water and the warmth of his skin coaxed her to hang on.

She stared at the strong column of his throat.

He made a move to throw her and she squealed again, wrapping her arms more securely around his neck.

In a quiet voice, he said, "I got you."

"I know." Her breath caught when she looked into his eyes. "You can let me down now."

Slowly, he did. Settling his hands at her waist, he said softly, "I'll never let you down, Annie."

Like a splash of cold water to the face, Annie frowned. "That's a lot of pressure."

"Maybe."

Part of being together for the long haul was giving each other slack and not expecting perfection. If they made it that far.

Absently running her palms down his strong arms, she grabbed his hands with hers and gave him a shake. "Don't put that on yourself, okay? Not for me."

His eyes narrowed. "Maybe we should agree right now to worry less and trust these feelings a little more."

She didn't know about that. Her feelings were running rampant lately. "How about we agree to worry less. For now."

"Deal." He leaned toward her with an intent look on his face.

Annie wasn't about to break their promise of *friendly* fun. She dove backward out of his reach, splashing as she went. "We're here to swim, remember?"

"Agreed." He dove forward and they swam farther out and then side by side in line with the shore.

He was a good swimmer but held back on her account. She'd never have been able to keep up had he lengthened his strokes.

"I'm going in to dry out and warm up." Shivering, she trudged out of the water, reached her towel and lay on her back.

It wasn't as comfortable as the sand beach in Maple Springs, but not bad. The stones were smooth and flat and warm and then there was the added bonus of no sand stuck all over. Crossing her ankles, she tipped her head up toward the sun and closed her eyes.

"Can you feel the baby move?" Matthew flopped on his stomach next to her.

She'd been absently rubbing her belly and stopped when she realized it was something she did a lot of lately. "Not yet."

He nodded toward her middle. "You've got a bump there. In the last couple of weeks you've popped out."

She'd noticed that, too. "It's not going to be easy to hide it much longer."

"Why hide it at all?"

Annie shrugged. They'd made an agreement not to worry, but she couldn't help it. She was already letting him down. "I want to make sure everything's okay."

"I know."

"Once everything checks out with the ultrasound at the doctor's office, I'll tell a few people, starting with Jack's parents."

He propped himself up on his elbows. "I want you to come with me to my parents' place Father's Day weekend for a cookout."

Father's Day was less than two weeks away. "I don't know."

"I've got to catch ship by the sixteenth, and I want you to meet my mom. I'd feel better knowing you had another person to call while I'm gone besides Jack's mom and Ginger. What if they're both out and you needed something?"

Annie chuckled. "That's what cell phones are for."

"My mom's had ten kids. She knows stuff. I want you to go." He was serious.

Meeting his family was a big step. What on earth would they think of her? And him? She rubbed her stomach again and felt an odd sensation of fluttering deep inside. "Whoa…"

"What?" He sat up, alarmed.

She smiled. Not moths this time, more like bird wings slapping a window. "I felt… I don't know. Something."

His eyes widened and he stretched his hand toward her, then hesitated. "Can I?"

"Umm, sure, but I don't think you'll feel anything." She tensed when Matthew gently touched her midsection. Heat from his palm radiated through the damp material of her top.

And then she felt it again. The flapping movement.

Her eyes filled and burned. Could her baby tell this touch wasn't hers? Her baby didn't know Jack was gone, but in time he'd wonder why he didn't have a father. A child deserved a father. A boy needed a dad.

She looked at Matthew. What was she doing? Their relationship could backfire and then what?

He quickly pulled his hand back. "Can't feel anything."

"It's early yet." Annie sat up and sniffed. No way would she cry.

He looked a little shaken, too.

Scared or sick, or a little of both, she couldn't tell but it made her laugh.

"What?"

Relieved to lighten this moment, she tossed a small pebble his way. "You look like you might pass out."

He caught it with one hand. "I won't. It's that, well, this just got real."

"Wait till you see the ultrasound pictures."

Matthew looked really scared then.

Annie laughed again. "You don't have to go. Seriously, Ginger already volunteered."

"I'm going. And I'd feel a lot better once you've met my mom." He sounded stern.

As he said, things were getting real, real quick. She was going to have a baby. She might not be able to do this all by herself. Would she truly be able to drive herself to the hospital when the time came?

Good advice from another woman who'd been through it many times over might be a good thing. "Okay, I'll go to your family cookout and meet your mom."

"Tired?" Matthew held open the passenger-side door of his truck for Annie.

They'd taken the last ferry ride back to Mackinac City before the sun had even set. He was tempted to suggest they drive the long way home, stop at Sturgeon Bay beach and watch the sun go down, but Annie's yawns had ruled that out.

"Yes. But a good tired. A fun tired." Her face was sunburned and rosy and her dark blond hair golden. "I'm going to sleep like a rock tonight."

Longing cut through him sharp and quick. "Good."

She buckled her seat belt and waited. "Are you going to get in?"

"Yeah." He moved away from the open door he'd been leaning against and circled the front of his truck, tapping the hood as he went.

When he climbed behind the wheel, he started the engine and cranked the air, but he didn't back out. Not yet. He'd had a great time today and didn't want it to end. He didn't want to drop her off and then head home. But he had to.

He turned in his seat. "Annie, let's do this again."

"Maybe when you're home in the fall, we can come back. It must be gorgeous with the colored leaves."

"That's not what I meant. I want to go out with you again, before I leave."

Her eyes widened.

"A date, Annie. I want to take you on a real date."

He'd made a commitment to be there for her and the baby. Maybe he shouldn't rush things, but he wanted to be sure. Would they mesh as well as he thought they could?

"Where do you want to go?"

"I don't know. Maybe Traverse City. We can grab dinner and look at stuff for the nursery."

Her eyes softened. "Friday evening might be best for that."

"Good. Then it's a date." Maybe they could do something else in between. He looked at her some more. With her ball cap off and her hair pulled up into a thick ponytail, she looked relaxed. Carefree even.

"What?" She tipped her head.

"You're really beautiful, did you know that?"

"Matthew..." her tone warned him to stay put.

Not going to happen.

He flipped the console between them up and out of the way and moved closer. "We're away from anyone who might tell."

"Yeah, but—"

Gently, he unbuckled her seat belt. "I'm going to kiss you, Annie. Right here, right now."

Her eyes widened, but she didn't refuse.

This time it wouldn't be about loss and angry grief. This time, he aimed to find out if what they had was real. If they could be more than simply friends sharing their sorrow.

Cupping her cheek, Matthew lowered his lips to hers. Awkward at first, he felt the tension leave Annie when she finally kissed him back. Sweet and filled with promise, Matthew knew where he stood. And what he wanted.

Pulling back, he searched her eyes. He didn't see any tears or regret. Only pleasant surprise and warmth.

"Thanks for a great day." He smiled.

She smiled back. "You're welcome."

And that's when he knew for sure.

He loved her.

Chapter Ten

Friday morning, Matthew strolled into the IGA store around the corner to pick up lunch to go. He and his brother Cam planned to spend a few hours fishing the bay on Cam's boat.

Matthew gave his order at the deli counter when he heard the telltale sound of a woman in high heels approaching behind him. He turned.

Holly Miller's eyes widened with interest. "Good morning, Matthew."

He gave her a nod. "Holly."

She peeked at the deli clerk engaged in making two sub sandwiches and grinned. "Looks like someone is planning a romantic picnic."

He grit his teeth at the lilt in her voice. He couldn't let the nosy woman get away with the wrong assumption. "Fishing with my brother."

"Ah…" That clearly wasn't the answer she'd hoped for. "So, how's Annie?"

Matthew hesitated. He'd like to set Holly straight about a few things when it came to him and Annie, but he wasn't about to lie. Especially since the gossip he believed she'd started had become true.

Tonight, he'd take Annie over an hour away from the prying eyes of Maple Springs for dinner. The other day, they'd gone out to breakfast, but tonight was their real date.

He looked at the young woman and challenged her. "What do you want to know?"

Holly's eyes widened and she shifted but didn't back down. "Well, considering that she's recently *widowed*, I wondered how she's dealing."

He didn't miss the dig of sarcasm in her voice. It was no one's business if they went out, but in a small town, people made it so. Eventually gossip died down on its own, but for Annie's sake, Matthew hoped to speed its death.

"She's having a hard time. We both are. Helping with that museum donation has been a great way to honor the man who was like another brother to me, so thanks for that."

Holly looked surprised at his compliment. "Oh, sure. You're welcome."

He'd scored a hit and went for home. "I worked with Jack for years. There isn't anyone I'd call a better friend."

"Oh." He'd taken the wind out of her sails a little with that statement. Good.

"I didn't realize you were so close."

"I'll do whatever I can to help Annie through this rough time. She deserves a little slack, don't you think?"

Holly's color deepened. "Yes, of course. Difficult situation."

She had no idea. Matthew received two wrapped subs and nodded to the clerk. "Thanks. Have a great day, Holly."

"You, too."

Matthew picked up a bag of chips, pop and then headed

for the cashier to pay. He added a bag of ice to his bill and looked up as Darren's ex-fiancée walked in.

He squarely met her gaze. Did she have any idea what she'd done to his brother? Did she even care?

She quickly looked away and kept walking.

Evidently not.

Matthew left, grabbing a bag of ice from the metal cooler outside. The women in this town could be petty and cruel. Darren stayed away because of it. The gossip grapevine had buzzed for months after his brother's breakup last year.

Small towns *talked*, but Maple Springs wasn't a regular small town. It was a resort community littered with wealthy summer residents and loads of tourists. The *beautiful people* also descended during the ski season. And a lot of regular, year-round folks put on judgmental airs to compete with those beautiful people. Or feel like part of them. Folks like Holly, who dared raise her eyebrows at Annie.

He got in his truck and slammed the door.

"What's with you?" His brother Cam adjusted the lid on his cup before taking a drink.

"Didn't you see Raleigh?" Matthew couldn't believe Cam missed their brother's ex-fiancée. She must have walked right in front of the truck.

"Who cares? Darren's better off without her." Cam raised his steaming coffee in mock toast. "Here's to staying single, right little brother?"

Matthew didn't answer.

He was lost in the memory of a camping trip with all his brothers right before Darren's wedding. Even their oldest brother, Zac, had made it on a rare furlough from active duty and they'd ribbed Darren pretty good. They vowed never to fall prey to the wedding wiles of women.

Spending time with Annie made Matthew realize he didn't want that toast. But a future with her was a two-for-one deal. He'd help raise Jack's child and that was a big responsibility. One that shouldn't be taken lightly.

Cam jerked his shoulder. "You're a goner, aren't you?"

"Huh?"

His brother laughed. "Never mind."

Matthew pulled out, ignoring the squeal of tires and the shocked look from Cam. His love for Annie wasn't only real, it was serious. The kind that might last forever.

Annie got out of her car, took a deep breath and waved. It sure felt as if she'd run away. And maybe that wasn't such a bad thing.

Matthew jogged toward her. "This is crazy, you know that."

"But it's fun. Here, you drive." She handed him her keys.

Meeting Matthew at the chain grocery store in the next town made sense. Her car got better gas mileage, and she didn't want his truck left sitting in her driveway until late tonight. Someone would certainly notice, and she didn't want to deal with all that. So here they were.

He opened the passenger-side door for her. "You look nice."

"Thanks. You said dress casual and bring a jacket." Annie fastened her seat belt over a pale purple summer knit dress she'd dug out of her closet. It had a shirred waist with a lot of give that comfortably hugged her thickening middle. She settled her purse and a cotton sweater in her lap.

Matthew slid behind the wheel and adjusted his seat. "Ready?"

She inhaled his subtle cologne and smiled. "Where are we going for dinner?"

"You'll see."

"By the way, you look nice, too." He wore a plain yellow oxford cloth shirt and khakis.

This wasn't a couple of old friends hanging out. This was a real date, and her stomach fluttered in anticipation of the evening ahead. Matthew didn't help calm her jitters as he refused to give her any clues to what he had planned.

Grilling him with questions ate up the hour-and-a-half drive to Traverse City. When they finally pulled into the parking lot of a certain marina, Annie grinned. "Wow, really?"

"I thought you might enjoy a dinner cruise on a tall ship like Jack's model. If this is good, we'll come back when the baby's older and can experience this, too."

Annie's eyes burned. Matthew was equal parts thoughtful and clueless. Making tonight about a future together touched her deeply, but his mention of Jack made it bittersweet.

She glanced at the wedding ring she still wore. She couldn't expect Matthew to leave Jack out of their relationship if she wasn't ready to let go. His willingness to keep Jack's memory alive for the sake of her baby was truly noble and good. But was this whole dating thing right for her? And more important, was it right for Matthew?

The following Friday, Annie took a deep breath and blew it back out. She paced, she silently counted, but nothing soothed. She peered out the window. No sign of Matthew's truck. It was early yet and nothing had kept her mind off the upcoming doctor's visit in the next town. Near where Jack's parents lived.

This was the big one. The appointment when she'd finally see her baby with an ultrasound and hopefully get news that everything was all right. With a good report, she'd tell people about the baby, starting with Jack's parents.

She chewed her bottom lip, dreading Marie's reaction. The woman would no doubt be in her face daily, checking on what she ate, how well she'd slept; even her bathroom habits would be open season for Jack's mom.

Annie shoved her hands in the pockets of linen drawstring pants. She wore loose and shapeless clothes in an attempt to hide her stomach. Despite dressing in the baggiest dancewear she could find, her baby bump was growing. She'd even received a few lingering glances.

She blew out another deep breath. It might be okay. Once the news that she was having a baby was out in the open, she could go back to wearing whatever she wanted. She'd even purchase real maternity clothes. Maybe she'd ask Marie to go with her on that shopping trip.

An image of a tent-shaped T-shirt with a ruffled collar flashed through her mind. Annie could imagine the kind of clothes Jack's mom might pick out, but going would mean a lot to Marie. This was her only grandchild, after all. Annie needed to build a solid relationship with her in-laws for her baby's sake. They were his only set of grandparents alive.

She heard Matthew's truck pull into her drive and smiled. Their outing to Mackinac Island the previous week had definitely started something. And since their dinner cruise date a week ago, they'd driven far from town for a picnic on the beach, and then again for a movie. They'd even browsed a hardware store nearly fifty miles away to check paint colors for the walls of her soon-to-be nursery.

Ginger called their meetings *clandestine*, but Annie had laughed and said they were simply fun. But that wasn't all they were. Annie was beginning to think that maybe, just maybe, a future with Matthew was possible.

Away from prying eyes and the expectations of their grief, she and Mathew relaxed. They enjoyed getting to know each other better on their own terms. Annie had done her best to keep those get-togethers light and easy, but Matthew's comment about sailing the tall ship one day as a real family filled her with hope. It also nagged at her conscience.

A quick knock and Matthew opened the door. "Ready?"

She clenched her hands into fists then shook them out, scattering her thoughts. "As ready as I'll ever be, I suppose."

"Nervous?"

Annie took a deep breath and let loose a soft laugh. "Ah, yeah."

He gave her a quick kiss. "It'll be okay."

She searched his eyes and then finally nodded. He couldn't promise her a safe tomorrow any more than Jack could.

She grabbed her purse and followed him out. The day was sunny and dry in the high seventies but nothing like the summer heat they'd had. This was normal weather for the middle of June.

Two days before Father's Day. Annie looked forward to giving Jack's dad the news about becoming a grandfather. Maybe she'd stop over Sunday after church and tell Jack's parents then.

And one day before Matthew's family picnic. The one

she'd agreed to go to with him. And that was another set of nerves waiting to happen.

Once in his truck, Matthew grabbed her hand and held it. "Maybe we should pray."

A great idea and something Annie often failed to do. "Yes, please."

Matthew bowed his head. "Lord, we trust You to protect Annie and the baby. And please show us the way. Amen."

"Amen." Annie gave his hand a squeeze before letting go. A simple prayer and yet he'd summed up everything rather well.

Matthew drove out of Maple Springs before he finally said, "Did you know that Jack used to say a similar prayer when he came on duty? Every day he'd ask God for protection and guidance."

"No, I didn't know."

"Good habit, to pray daily, don't you think?"

"Yes." Annie knew that it was, but she'd fallen away from seeking God. Afraid to really trust Him because He'd taken Jack away from her.

And now there was Matthew. What did God think about that? Annie hadn't really asked and certainly hadn't listened for an answer. There was always the possibility that she might not like what she heard.

Matthew wasn't sure what he'd been thinking coming here. He couldn't even pace the waiting room. He'd been given the evil eye by the receptionist to sit back down and behave. He knew Annie needed his support, but waiting while she met with her doctor privately had tied him up in knots.

Was she hearing good news or bad?

By the time someone came to get him for the ultrasound, he'd nearly hit the restroom to toss his breakfast. He'd never expected baby stuff might get to him like this. He'd never expected Annie would, either. But when he stepped into the exam room with Annie stretched out on the table with fear shimmering in her eyes, he knew why he'd come.

"Hey." He grabbed her hand.

She gave him a wobbly smile and squeezed hard. "Hey."

"You can sit beside her, there." The technician pointed to a chair out of the way next to Annie's head.

He did as instructed and silently watched while the tech put gel on Annie's bare midsection. Then she followed with a wand that hooked into a computer.

"Relax. This will be a breeze." The tech patted Annie's hand.

Then the show began and Matthew was blown away. There on the screen, the baby moved and even sucked its thumb. "Would you look at that?"

He glanced at Annie.

She had tears streaming down her cheeks and a rapt expression on her face.

The tech continued to explain what they saw. The baby's arm, the heartbeat, stomach—and then she stopped. "Would you like to know what you're having?"

Annie didn't hesitate. "Yes. Definitely yes!"

The tech didn't bother looking at him. Annie had told him that her doctor's office knew about Jack's death. And she'd cleared either his or Ginger's presence ahead of time for this test.

"Congratulations. It looks like a boy."

Annie laughed. "I knew it!"

By the time the doctor came in to go over the findings and measurements, Matthew was thinking ahead. Way ahead. Jack would want his boy to know how to fish and maybe play sports.

He ran a hand through his hair. It'd be up to him to show Jack's boy those things. He couldn't blow it with Annie and then not be around for Jack's son.

After Annie's doctor jotted down notes in her chart, the woman smiled. "Everything looks really good, Annie. I'm very pleased. I see no reason for alarm, but I'll order another ultrasound as we get closer, maybe even two. But you are doing great and so is your son. Keep doing what you're doing."

Annie returned with a smile of her own that couldn't be broader. "My son. I love the sound of that. Thank you."

By the end of the appointment, Annie was given several glossy pictures taken during the ultrasound. Some of them were difficult to figure out, but it wasn't hard to see how Annie's features softened as she ran her fingers across the paper before putting the bundle of images in her purse.

"Your little boy," Matthew said.

"And Jack's." She looked up at him. "This little guy will be a third."

Matthew chuckled. "Carrying on the Marshall tradition?"

"Absolutely."

"He might even become a freighter captain like his dad and granddad before him." Matthew grinned.

Annie smiled back. "If he wants to be."

Matthew wrapped an arm around Annie's shoulders and gave her a squeeze. "Congratulations. If you've got time before class, I think we should celebrate with lunch."

A shadow crossed over Annie's features. "Can we make it quick? I need to get to the studio soon."

"There's a deli right across the street." Matthew pointed. "They have awesome pies and brownies, too."

"Good, because I'm hungry."

A healthy baby was reason enough to celebrate, but the look in Annie's eyes, the relief he saw there as well as excitement and anticipation, were icing on the cake. They dashed across the busy street and Matthew kept his arm around Annie. Drawing her close to his side, he kissed her temple.

Once across the street, she stopped walking and placed her hand on his chest. "Thank you."

"For what?"

Her eyes looked bluer than the sky overhead. "For helping me through this."

Words seemed inadequate, so he leaned down and kissed her. When Matthew heard a gasp, he pulled back to see what the fuss was about.

Marie Marshall had come out of the deli with a boxed pie in her hands that teetered precariously.

He stepped forward to help, but the woman righted the box and backed away.

Then she turned on Annie. "How dare you!"

"Marie…" Annie's face blazed and her hands went to her middle, as if protecting Jack's boy from the shrill indignation in his grandmother's voice.

"Jack's not even cold in the ground and you're parading around like a…like a…" Marie's voice carried and folks passing by stared.

Matthew reached his hand out to her. "Why don't we go inside where we can talk?"

"I will not sit at the same table with you!" Marie hissed. She narrowed her gaze and nearly bore holes into Annie's midsection when she went pale.

"Matthew, go in and order for me. I'll be a moment."

Annie looked ready to do battle.

He didn't leave. "I don't think I should."

"No. It's okay." Annie gave him a nod and then reached into her purse and pulled out the ultrasound images. "Marie, you had better sit down. There's something I have to tell you."

Jack's mom sort of crumpled onto one of two benches stationed in front of the deli.

Annie sat next to her, but she glanced at him and nodded again for him to go inside.

Matthew headed toward the entrance. He'd give the two women privacy, but the deli had a wall of windows with spectacular views of the bay and them. He'd keep watch. And run back outside if needed.

From inside, he couldn't make out what Annie said, but she gave Jack's mom the ultrasound images. Marie sat ramrod-straight and Matthew knew that rigid posture didn't bode well for Annie. Not well at all.

Annie held her tongue while Marie looked over each image of the baby. She wanted to give her time to process and accept the news. And hopefully forgive her for keeping it from her.

"So, you're finally having a baby. Is it *his*?" Marie gestured toward the deli.

It would have hurt less if she'd been whipped. "This baby is Jack's son. Your grandson."

Marie's eyes grew cold. "Are you lying to cover up your sin?"

"No! Marie, why would you think that?"

"It's what anyone would think. It's what everyone *will* think if you keep carrying on with that man."

Annie's defenses rose. "That man has a name. Matthew. And he's been a dear friend of Jack's and mine for years. Our shared grief brought us closer, and yes, it's more than friendship now. Why is that so terrible?"

Marie shook her head as if she were a lost cause and stupid besides. "Because you dishonor Jack by taking up with another so soon after his death. It's not right, Annie. Search your soul, and you'll know it's true."

Annie took the paper images from Marie's hands. "I'm sorry you feel that way."

Marie stood and looked down at her.

It was the same disapproving glare she'd given her when Jack first brought her home to meet his parents. Annie had never done anything right in her mother-in-law's eyes. Why did she expect understanding now? But was congratulations too much to ask? A little joy even?

"Why did you keep this from me if the baby is Jack's?" Real pain shone from Marie's eyes. And disappointment.

Annie swallowed hard. "I'm considered high-risk. I was afraid I might not carry past the first few months. I couldn't bear to share the news only to then lose this baby. I couldn't tell you until I was sure this little guy would be okay."

Marie's eyes filled with tears. "A boy? When?"

"Mid November." Annie held her breath and waited. Hoping…

Marie finally nodded, and then lifted her chin. "Think about what I said. Think about Jack and the respect you owe his memory."

Annie slumped as she watched her walk away. The sun shimmered off the lake, but the beauty that lay before her didn't matter. She had hoped for a chance to finally bond with such precious news, but Marie had spurned her instead. The worst part of it was Annie's chastened heart burned.

Marie might be right.

Annie buried her face in her hands and wept.

Matthew handed her a bundle of napkins. He carried a brown paper bag in the other hand. "I got everything to go. Why don't we eat down by the lake?"

Annie blew her nose. "I'm not sure I can right now."

"Try," he said softly and offered his hand. "Come on."

She took it and stood but felt like her body might shake apart.

Matthew wrapped his arm around her. "Tell me what happened with Marie."

"It's nothing." That was so not true. Marie had lanced her heart with her words. "Just the usual disapproval."

"Seems like more than that. Do you want me to talk to her?"

"No!" She let loose a bitter laugh. The last thing she wanted Matthew to hear was Marie's accusations.

They walked across the street and down a paved path to a park overlooking the bay. A few cars were parked and several people had walked, jogged or biked past them on the path that followed around the bay back to Maple Springs.

A family had already set up for a picnic under the pavilion. Two small children weaved through empty picnic tables as their dad tried to corral them into order. The mom seemed oblivious and unpacked a cooler.

Matthew led them farther away to a solitary picnic table shaded by a huge maple tree.

Annie followed, numb.

He emptied the brown bag and handed her a foil bundle. "I ordered you a veggie sandwich."

"Thanks." She watched him unwrap his sandwich, marveling at the stack of deli meat stuffed between the bread. He then laid out two different slices of pie, a brownie and a chocolate chip cookie on the picnic table. Right between them.

"What's with all the sweets?"

"I wasn't sure what you'd like, so I got a little of everything. Whatever we don't eat, I'll take home for Luke. The kid eats everything in sight."

Annie's stomach rumbled. She hadn't had much of a breakfast, and she really needed something to get her through hours of dance class. She checked her watch. They were cutting it close.

"Everyone grieves differently, right?" Matthew asked after they'd recited the Zelinsky family prayer.

"I suppose." She waited for him to finish chewing. "Why? What's your point?"

"My point is that Marie grieves. You're the one who took Jack away from her and now he's gone for good. So she's lashing out."

Annie tamped down her anger. "We were married for fifteen years. She should have learned to share."

Matthew dipped his head. "True. But she's not exactly a warm, fuzzy person and Jack was her only kid. Her boy. Jack wouldn't want a shrine, but Marie expects you to give him one."

He didn't know the unforgiveable things Marie had said. "Why are you defending her, Matthew?"

"I'm not. My guess is that she's acting out of hurt and you shouldn't take what she says to heart."

Annie snorted. Dear, kind Matthew would look at things that way. In fact, he sounded a lot like Jack. How many times had her husband coached her through wanting to tear her hair out over some insensitive dig Marie had made?

Finally, she sighed. "I'll try."

She'd give Marie some slack and go over on Sunday as she'd planned. Maybe then, after some time to think, they could sit down and talk rationally. Maybe then, there'd be some joy over the news of a baby. A baby she vowed to share.

Chapter Eleven

The next day, Annie gripped the seat belt while Matthew drove to his parents' house northeast of town. They drove inland past farmland, open fields and rolling hills. Away from the tourists and summer residents of Maple Bay. Away from any whispers.

Not far enough to escape Marie's words. Similar words had been echoed by a couple of clients picking up their kids from ballet class the day before. One woman asked when she was due and then beat around the bush for the date of Jack's death as if trying to figure it out. Marie had been right and it had plagued her all night long.

Annie shifted in the seat. Soon, she'd meet Matthew's family. Would they wonder whose child she carried?

Matthew rubbed her knee. "You okay? You're awfully quiet."

"A little nervous to meet your whole family."

Matthew chuckled. "Not everyone will be there. Not Zac or Cat, but enough of us, I suppose. Don't worry. They're nice people."

"I can't imagine them being anything but." Annie twined her fingers with Matthew's and held on.

Of course his family would be nice. Matthew's suggestion of his mom as a possible resource was a good one and the reason she'd agreed to come today. Another person to ask questions in case Marie refused to talk to her. Annie's sister was far away in Arizona, and although Ginger was nearby, she had little experience with babies.

They pulled into the driveway that led to a huge log-style home, and Annie remembered picking up Jack here once. Then, the small inland lake had been covered in snow like an open field. Today, the water glimmered in the sunshine. Inviting and peaceful.

She could use some peace right about now.

"There aren't many neighboring homes." Annie looked around. The next house over was a good mile away.

"Growing up, I hated how isolated it was out here. I'd catch a ride into town every chance I could. Or ride my bike if nothing else worked out."

"Must have been a long bike ride."

"Oh, it was." Matthew shut off the engine then pointed. "There's the sugar shack where our maple syrup is made."

A small barn, sided the same as the house, stood several hundred feet away. "You think I could get a tour?"

"My dad would love that. He's proud of his syrup operation."

"With good reason." Annie got out and stretched.

Maybe coming here would be okay. Maybe she was making too much of what Marie had said. But then, maybe not.

"I'm so glad you're here." The tall, older woman had to be Matthew's mom. She hustled toward them and her frosted-blond bob swished forward with each step.

"Mom, this is Annie Marshall."

"Of course it is. I remember you well, dear." She smiled.

Annie smiled back and extended her hand. "Hi, Mrs. Zelinsky."

"Oh, no, you must call me Helen." Then she enveloped her into a warm hug and whispered, "I'm so sorry about Jack."

Annie wrestled with the urge to hang on tight. There was something warm and accepting about Matthew's mom. Something strong, too. "Thank you."

Helen pulled back but kept her arm around Annie's shoulders. "Darren just started the grill, so it'll be a little while before we eat. Can I get you some lemonade or herbal iced tea?"

"Tea, please."

"She wants a tour of the sugar shack." Matthew walked behind them.

"Andy will be ecstatic." Helen opened the screen door with a soft creak. "He also loves that desk you gave him. Thank you for that."

"I was glad to see it go. Heavy thing. I could never move it around myself."

Helen laughed. "Then you'll understand why it's where it is. Come in and relax and then Andy will show you the shack."

Matthew's father came out of the kitchen and introduced himself. Tall and distinguished-looking with broad shoulders and keen blue eyes, Andy Zelinsky had a stern jaw and air of authority. His sons resembled him.

"You'd like to see the syrup operation?'

"I would." Annie glanced at Matthew. Would he go, too?

Matthew gave her an encouraging smile.

"Let's go." Andy nodded toward the door.

"Give her a minute to drink her iced tea," Helen scolded.

"She can bring it with her."

"Andy…"

Annie raised her hand. "I'll take that iced tea to go if that's okay?"

Helen handed over an insulated tumbler filled to the top. "I'll put Matthew to work in here."

"Great." Matthew groaned. "I think I'd rather hit the tour."

Helen gave her son a pointed look. "Your sisters aren't here yet and neither is Luke or Cam. Darren's got grill duty."

Matthew surrendered. "Okay, okay. What can I do?"

Annie sipped the tea quickly to keep it from spilling over. It was obvious that Helen wanted to talk to her son. Maybe even about her. That thought made Annie's stomach pitch. One thing she'd noticed about Matthew's mom was that she had shrewd eyes. Helen Zelinsky saw too much.

She turned to Matthew's dad. "Ready when you are."

Andy smiled. The same easy smile as his son. He gave his wife a nod. "We won't be long."

Annie followed him out across an expanse of freshly cut green lawn warmed by the sun. Her flip-flops slapped against the soles of her feet. Really quiet way out here, and so different from the gentle hum in town.

She spotted flower beds that bordered parts of the yard before turning into a forest of maple trees dotted with evergreens. "Beautiful property you have."

"We think so, too."

It wasn't a long walk before they came to the windowed barn.

"It's a small operation, but we like it that way. My daughter Monica wants me to market online with a catalogue and shipping, but Helen and I enjoy the craft fair circuit. We're content with that. For now." Andy opened a garage-like door with a rattle and snap.

Annie gaped when she stepped inside. Beautiful rough sewn wood and shining stainless steel greeted her. A stack of metal buckets and boxes of plastic jugs lined one wall. Clean and tidy. "Wow."

Andy patted the top of the desk she'd given him. "This is perfect for keeping track of batches. I plan to store journals of each year's yield in these drawers. Nice and sturdy. It'll hold up."

Annie smiled. "I think Jack would be proud. It's no heirloom, just something he picked up at a garage sale. So don't worry if it gets ruined."

Matthew's father looked thoughtful. "Helen and I are very sorry for your loss. A loss to all of us. Jack was a good man. And Matthew took his death hard."

But he'd been a pillar of strength for her ever since he came home. They'd talked only once while he was out on the lakes after Jack's funeral. One evening while in port, Matthew had called her. They hadn't said much, but something about being on the line with him, even silent, had helped.

"Thank you," Annie whispered. "It hasn't been easy."

Matthew's parents were not awkward about Jack's death. They expressed sympathy with open sincerity and waited for her to change the subject instead of rushing ahead before she might add something uncomfortable. Share some painful memory.

"It never is." Andy got a faraway look in his eyes.

Matthew's father had retired from a long career in the military. She couldn't remember which branch, but he'd no doubt experienced loss, as well.

"Your son's friendship has helped me through this. He gets it better than most." Annie went out on a limb and added, "You look like you know what I mean."

Andy nodded. His expression bespoke understanding. "Lost a good man under my command. My closest friend."

"I'm sorry. But that doesn't really cover it, does it?"

"No. But thank you just the same." Andy's gaze never wavered. His past grief was plain to see.

The pain never went away. It dulled over time but remained. She'd lost her parents and buried herself in dance, but that didn't mean it hadn't affected her. The pain of losing Jack would remain, too.

"You've been good for Matthew." In Andy's eyes she read hope.

She tipped her head. "How?"

"By focusing on you, he stopped asking why."

Feeling her throat tighten, she whispered, "Those *whys* can be killers."

"And drag a person into a black hole without care."

So far, Annie had stayed out of that hole. And maybe plodding through was part of her problem. People had expected more despair from her. But what good would any of that do? Jack wasn't coming home. Life went on, right along with the pain.

She tipped her head. "So how do you make the syrup?"

Andy chuckled. "I'll give you our *educational* tour."

Annie finally relaxed, glad that she'd come.

"Here, put these on a plate would you?" His mom handed him a plastic container of cut-up veggies. "And wash your hands."

Matthew grabbed a plate from the cupboard and then washed his hands as told. Dumping the veggies on the plate, he snatched a radish. "Do you have any dip?"

"In the fridge." His mom elbowed him out of the way. "I could have done that. Arrange them a little, see?"

"No one's going to care." He grabbed a celery stick.

"When is Annie due?" His mom fiddled with the veggies and didn't look at him.

"How'd you know?" Matthew didn't think Annie's baby bump showed under the billowy shirt she wore over a pair of long shorts.

His mom looked up. "I've had enough kids of my own to tell." Then her gaze narrowed in on him. "Your doing?"

"What!" Matthew inhaled a bit of radish and coughed.

"You've known each other a long time. Sometimes things happen when grief's involved." Her voice dipped low and soft.

He knew that tone. The many times he'd gotten in trouble as a kid, she'd use that tone trying to sound understanding before taking a switch to his backside. "No, Mom. No."

He ran a hand through his hair. "There's nothing to repent over, okay? Annie's due around the middle of November, and Jack will never know his own son."

His mom's shoulders relaxed and she counted on her fingers. Her eyebrows rose. "She's hardly showing at all for four and half months along."

He shrugged. "I don't know about that, but we went for the ultrasound yesterday."

His mom's head popped up from her task of arranging cut vegetables. "We? You went, too?"

He grabbed another celery stick and bit into it with a snap. "Yeah. And it was pretty amazing…" He stopped talking at the look of awe on his mother's face. "What?"

She smiled. Big and wide. "You're in love with her, aren't you?"

Love. Warmth spread through him at hearing the word spoken aloud. He'd never admitted his feelings to anyone. Wasn't sure he should even now.

Then his mom's face fell into a thoughtful expression. "Now what?"

"Oh, Matty, she's dealing with a lot of emotions right now. Between her hormones and grief, Annie's a walking bundle of vulnerability."

Not to mention fears about losing her baby. But those had eased after the ultrasound. It wasn't his place to share that information with his mom, but he'd hoped Annie might, in time. "So what are you saying?"

His mom wiped her hands with a towel and stepped close to him, gripping his forearms. "You can't tell her how you feel. Not yet. It's too soon. You don't want to push her into something she's not ready for. Nor do you want to scare her away. You've got to be sure. You both do."

Not exactly a news flash, but not what he wanted to hear, either. He searched his mom's eyes, hoping she'd say something else. She didn't.

That next step had to wait. He had to wait. Annie worried too much about the rumor mill in Maple Springs. And he worried about Annie. Meeting outside of town for dates was crazy, but he'd agreed because it helped her relax. She claimed to have lost clients because of their relationship, so he'd gone along.

Maybe Annie's feelings weren't as strong as his. Their runaway dates were proof that she wasn't ready to face what they'd become. What they could be.

"I'm sorry, honey." His mom patted his hand and then looked up when the sliding door opened.

"The grill's ready," Darren said. "Hey, Matthew."

His mom grabbed a tray of hamburger patties, hot dogs and bratwurst and shoved it into his hands. "Go help your brother. The girls just pulled in and they can help me in here."

Matthew nodded.

His mother's advice settled in his gut like a lead anchor. How was he supposed to sink his feelings and not let them show?

"You look worried." Darren took the tray from him.

Matthew shrugged. "I'm fine."

"Right."

"Why don't you stick with grilling." Matthew spotted Annie walking toward them with his dad.

She carried a half-gallon bottle of maple syrup and laughed at his parents' cat that followed. Tigger attacked the back of Annie's flip-flops then rolled in the grass only to repeat an attack after she'd gotten ahead of him.

He caught up with her and reached for the jug, caressing her arm before covering her hand with his. "I'll put this in the house till we leave."

She smiled up at him but didn't let go. "I'll do it. I want to see if your mom needs help."

Matthew searched her face for what, he wasn't sure. But he was suddenly afraid of letting her out of his sight. "Okay."

He watched her enter the house and felt the cat twine around his ankles. He leaned down and scratched behind his ears. "What do you want, Mr. Tiggs?"

His dad slapped his back. "Help me set up the horseshoe pit."

Matthew followed. His father hadn't made a request.

When they were halfway across the yard, his father finally spoke. "Your mom thinks you're serious about this woman."

"I am." No use denying it. Matthew braced for whatever might come next.

His father might be a quiet man. A reverent man who'd punished them for throwing slices of bread at the dinner table when they were kids, but his words carried a ton of weight. "You think you can handle living with the shadow of her first husband?"

Matthew cocked his head. "I think so."

"Memories of Jack will always be part of your lives together."

"I don't expect her to forget him." He wouldn't, either.

"That's good. She won't stop loving him, and you can't expect her to."

"I loved him, too, Dad." Matthew glanced at his father. "Mom thinks it's too soon."

His dad only shrugged. "Maybe it is."

"Maybe it's not," Matthew finished.

"What's your hurry?"

Matthew blew out his breath. Watching Annie walk into her house all alone at night was part of it. He wanted to give her security and the assurance that she wasn't alone. That he'd be there to help raise her boy. He wanted the freedom to love her. "I don't know."

His father folded his arms. "You're smart enough to make good decisions, but it's wise to pray for direction. Just don't forget to listen for the answer."

Right. "Thanks, Dad."

"I mean it."

"I know. You're right."

As Matthew added more sand to the horseshoe pits, he heard the words Jack prayed at the start of each morning shift. Matthew wanted that same quiet assurance that came from knowing what lay ahead and being prepared for it. Maybe he and Annie needed more time to know where to go from here. And God was the only one who could truly guide their steps.

He only hoped he had ears enough to hear.

* * *

"Can I help?" Annie entered the sunny kitchen that opened up into a family room. The views were lovely. The massive backyard ended with a small sandy beach at the edge of the lake.

"Annie, these are two of my daughters, Monica and Erin."

Both young women were tall and beautiful and munching on chocolate chip cookies from a plastic-wrapped plate that had been broken into.

"Want one?" Monica lifted the plate.

"No." Annie smiled. "But thank you."

Monica shrugged her shoulders and looked away.

Annie's stomach dropped. Great. She'd insulted her by not taking one.

Matthew's mom stepped forward and draped her arm around Annie's shoulders. "The girls have everything under control here. Come, I'll give you a tour and show you where the bathrooms are."

"Oh. Okay. Thanks." Annie would have asked, but Matthew's mom seemed excited to show her so she followed her from room to room. A big house, it took a while.

"Have you lived here long?" Annie finally asked.

Helen Zelinsky laughed. "Nearly my whole life. Andy and I were both born and raised in Maple Springs. We bought this place right after we married. I traveled some when he was stationed overseas, even after I had Zachary and Darren. But once Cameron was born, I came back here. I wanted a home base for my children. Something constant that wouldn't ever change. We've added on over the years, but it's still the same house. The same land."

Annie couldn't imagine raising that many little people into productive adults. One baby scared her enough and

Helen had managed ten, probably by herself a lot of the time. "Was your husband gone a lot, then?"

Helen nodded. "Yes. But then he'd come home on leave or I'd pack up the kids and go to him for a while. We managed."

Annie bit back a question.

Helen saw right through that and stopped to face her. "What's on your mind?"

"Were you ever afraid?"

Helen laughed again. "Of course, that's part of being a mom. I pray for my kids every day and always have, but I flew by the seat of my pants a lot of times, too."

Annie nodded. Would prayer be enough to raise Jack's son into the man he should be?

Matthew's mom draped her arm around Annie's shoulder again for a quick squeeze. "You'll do fine, Annie."

She knew.

Annie opened her mouth to ask how, but nothing came out.

"Matthew didn't tell me. I guessed. I can tell."

"With ten of your own, I suppose it was easy. The ultrasound made things very real. I'm not sure I know how to be a mom, but Jack would have made a great dad."

"Love covers a lot of mistakes."

Annie's eyes burned and then her cheeks. She didn't want to cry. Especially not in front of a woman who had raised kids on her own while her husband was in harm's way. Helen would think her a total wimp.

"It's okay to feel, Annie. Our weakness gives God the chance to show His strength. Lean on Him."

She sniffed and nodded. She had to stop leaning on Matthew with the expectation that he'd make things okay. That he'd take Jack's place.

"And you can call me any time you need to. I'm serious about that."

Tears welled again and ran over. Matthew had been right. She needed his mom. Maybe now more than ever. She managed a raw-sounding "Thanks."

Helen smiled and handed her a tissue from one of the bathrooms. "If you need to freshen up, take your time. I smell the food on the grill, so it's got to be ready. I better get down there. We can talk more later."

"Okay." Annie blew her nose and headed for the bathroom.

Once back downstairs, Annie helped Matthew's sisters take covered dishes out onto the deck through the slider in the family room. Passing by a wall covered with family photos, Annie stopped and stared. There, in the middle of a grouping of pictures, was one of a teenaged Matthew bottle-feeding a small raccoon.

Jack had shaken his head when he'd told her about the seagull with a broken wing that Matthew had mended. Even teased by the crew, Matthew hadn't given up, and before they put into port, the seagull had flown away. Healed.

Monica stood next to her. "He found that baby after its mom had been hit by a car. He nursed it, fed it and then finally released it."

"Even then," Annie whispered.

Monica chuckled. "He was always bringing home something or someone. Matthew never had to be coaxed into helping the elderly lady down the road after her husband died. My dad used to force us to go over there, but not Matthew. He'd go on his own. He's always had a soft spot for orphans and—ah, anything injured."

Annie nodded, but something twisted deep inside. Was she one of Matthew's projects? Monica hadn't said it, but she'd meant *widows*. Orphans and widows. Not that there was anything wrong with Matthew's compassion, but she'd been lapping up his kindness like a water-starved dog.

Their attraction was undeniable, but would it last? This heady need for each other had been born out of grief. Their first kiss had everything to do with desperation. But not the last few. The kisses they'd recently shared held promise. Even hope.

Annie set a bowl of potato salad on the huge picnic table that took up half the deck. When she looked up, Matthew stood across from her, looking back. His dark blue eyes shone with concern. He cared. He'd always cared.

Her heart tore a little.

Matthew deserved someone whole, someone who could stand on her own. And right now, that wasn't her.

Chapter Twelve

His family gathered around the picnic table for the meal-time prayer. Matthew echoed his father's words along with the rest of his family. They knew the drill. Not one piece of food until after they'd prayed.

"Amen." A family chorus rang out. It was always louder than the actual prayer and then dinner was attacked from all sides.

Matthew slid next to Annie and smiled.

She smiled back. But she didn't say anything. In fact, she'd been quiet all day.

Matthew was used to big family dinners but Annie wasn't. He and his siblings had filled their plates in no time as dishes were passed. He looked at Annie's pile of carrot and celery sticks and small plop of potato salad and chuckled. She was a rookie.

"Are you feeling okay?"

"Yeah, why?"

He had the tray of cheeseburgers in his hand and she was definitely eyeing one. "For starters, you look like you want one of these."

Annie frowned. "Actually, I do."

"You're kidding, right?"

"They smell so good." Annie took a cheeseburger and bit right into it. Then she sighed. "Taste good, too," she mumbled and took another bite.

Matthew openly stared. "Annie Marshall eating red meat. I never thought I'd see it."

She swallowed and then whispered, "Weird craving."

Matthew laughed. "Well, well. Now, that's my boy!"

Monica dropped her fork with a clatter against her plate. His sister's eyes grew round as portholes as she stared at Annie. "You're going to have a baby?"

The sudden silence surrounding the table slapped him hard. He'd let he news out of the bag. His family stared. At him and then at Annie.

Her face flamed. "Yes, but—"

His sister's gaze skewered him. "Matthew!"

"No, no," Annie stammered. "It's not…"

He looked at the stunned faces staring at him, waiting for an explanation. The narrowing of his father's eyes, the regret shining from Darren's, the smirk in Luke's. Even Cam looked surprised. Ben and Marcus were confused, but that was normal.

Matthew threw his hands in the air. "Whoa, whoa, wait. This is Jack's boy."

"Could be Jack's girl." His mom's cheerful voice broke through the awkwardness. "And very exciting, too. Wonderful news, Annie."

"Thank you, Mrs. Zelinsky."

He heard a collective sigh of relief. Or maybe he simply felt the tension lessen, but not from Annie. Her shoulders slumped with defeat. She wouldn't look at him, either.

Great. He'd botched that one.

He waited mere seconds for Annie to confirm the baby's gender and when she didn't, he did that, as well.

"We found out at the ultrasound appointment yesterday. He's definitely a boy."

Annie's eyes closed briefly. She settled her half eaten cheeseburger on her plate and nodded. "Yes, a boy."

Monica looked at Annie and then bore more holes into him, before shifting back to Annie. "Congratulations."

"Yeah, congrats. When are you due?" His sister Erin was all smiles.

"Mid November." Annie's voice wavered.

What was the big deal? Annie planned to tell folks, anyway. But then maybe she didn't want anyone to know she'd have a boy and he'd stepped on her toes making the announcement. But this was his family, not a group of strangers. Still, it was Annie's news to tell. Not his own.

He glanced at his brothers. Cam shifted in his seat, and Darren hung his head. Not even his younger brothers looked comfortable with the news. Except for Luke. His little brother bit into a bratwurst, completely unconcerned.

"It's probably too early to plan, but maybe we can host a shower for you here at the house. But we can talk more, closer to your date." His mother had given not only her approval, but her support, as well.

He could have hugged her right then and there.

Annie looked surprised, no, moved. And grateful. "Thank you."

Matthew reached for her hand under the table, encouraged when she threaded her fingers through his and held on.

They'd be okay. Waiting would be made easier by the fact that he'd be out on the lakes for the next few months. All he had to do was keep his mouth shut about how he felt until after he came back.

* * *

After a long and leisurely paced dinner, Matthew's sisters cleared the table, so Annie stood and gathered plates. So did Helen.

"Mom, sit, we got it," Monica said.

Helen made a face and nodded Annie's way. "I'll start a fire, then."

Annie watched Matthew's mom walk away. The guys had already left the table for the horseshoe pits. It was still pretty warm, but with clear skies and a distinct lack of humidity, the evening would no doubt grow cooler and a fire would be welcome.

She glanced at her watch. Seven-thirty. The sun wouldn't set for another two hours. Lifting a stack of scraped plates, she headed for the kitchen.

"Oh, here, let me take those." Erin reached for them.

Annie shook her head. "No worries, I have them. I'm not an invalid yet."

Erin laughed. "No. I guess you're not. You're a dancer right?"

Annie set the stack of plates on the counter. "An instructor now, but yes, I was. I own Marshall's Movement."

"Nice. I've heard you give some great classes there." Erin gave her a sweet smile. "No wonder you have an awesome figure."

"Thanks." Annie chuckled. She'd always been too thin for an *awesome* figure. "Not for long, though."

Monica's gaze wasn't so sweet. She had a protective gleam in her eyes that made Annie nervous. "Will you stop your classes then?"

Annie shrugged. "I hope to work as long as possible, with my doctor's approval. Classes slow down toward the holidays. I'm not working with the community dance theatre this year, so the timing is right."

Monica rinsed and loaded the dishwasher while Erin hunted for plastic containers to store the leftovers. "So, you waited quite a while then, huh?"

"Monica!" Erin looked horrified at such a personal question. She patted her hand. "You don't have to answer that."

Annie didn't miss the hint about her age. "It's okay. Jack and I tried for years, but nothing happened before... this."

The hard stare softened. "I'm sorry for your loss. I met your husband once when he was here with Matthew. Seemed like a really nice guy."

"He was." Her heart burned.

"You've known Matthew a long time. I guess it's no wonder you've grown closer." Monica looked straight through Annie as if reading the book of her soul and not liking its secrets.

Annie didn't flinch. "Your brother's a good friend."

Monica nodded, clearly not believing that answer.

Annie retreated for the last stack of plates.

Erin followed with a tray to gather up the condiments and gently touched her arm. "Don't mind her. She and Matthew have always been tight. Marcus, too, I suppose. The three M's of the family."

"Oh, no, it's fine." What else could she say? That she got it? Matthew's family wanted someone else for him, someone younger who could give him a whole houseful of kids.

Monica joined them and gathered up a bunch of glasses. "Thanks for helping. We usually wait a little while before serving dessert."

Annie held her belly. "No worries there. I'm stuffed."

"Me, too," Erin echoed. "I hope you like strawberry-rhubarb pie."

"I do." Not that she made a habit of eating sweets, but a small slice wouldn't hurt. She'd already wolfed down half of a cheeseburger.

"Good, because Mom makes the best." Erin gave her a conspiring wink. "And its Matthew's favorite."

"Good to know." Annie pretended to tuck that knowledge away for future reference.

"We're pretty much done here, if you want to go relax or play horseshoes." Monica latched the dishwasher and hit the on switch. "We team up and play against each other hoping to beat Dad."

"I'm not much of a horseshoe thrower, but I'd love to sit by the fire."

Monica looked relieved. She obviously didn't want Annie anywhere near their family tradition. "Make yourself comfortable. I'll tell Matthew."

Annie nodded and made her escape.

Finding the perfect chair near the fire pit, Annie plunked down. Helen had joined the rest at the horseshoe pits along the side yard near the tree line, so Annie was relatively alone.

A welcome relief, too. Ten minutes later, she still stared into the flames of the campfire, gathering her thoughts. The metallic clinks and clangs of horseshoes lulled her into a sleepy state, but she didn't close her eyes. For the first time in over a month, they were finally wide-open. And she knew what needed done.

Later, though. She stretched out her legs onto the Adirondack-style lounge and yawned.

"Tired?" Matthew leaned over her.

Her pulse skittered. "Yeah."

"Monica said you weren't interested in horseshoes. I could use a partner. Or would you rather head for home?"

Dear, kindhearted Matthew. She didn't want to take

him away from his family, or deny him a slice of his favorite pie. With Matthew and his siblings wrapped up in their horseshoe tournament, she wouldn't have to answer any more questions about the baby.

"You go ahead. I'm fine right here. I might even close my eyes."

He rubbed her shoulder. "Everything okay?"

It wasn't, but now wasn't the time for all that. "I'm a little sleepy. Need-a-short-nap sleepy, not done-for-the-night, you know?"

He hesitated and then stripped off the long-sleeve shirt he wore over a T-shirt. He draped it over her and then braced his hands on the armrests of the chair. "So you don't get cold."

Glancing up into his eyes, her heart broke. "Thanks."

He looked troubled, too, like he wanted to say something. "Annie..."

She managed a smile. "Don't keep your family waiting."

He leaned closer and gave her a featherlight kiss. "Have a good nap."

The thickness in her throat made it impossible to respond, so she nodded. As she watched him walk back to his family, Annie knew their brief kiss had been seen. It didn't matter. No one had bought into the claim that they were just friends, anyway.

And everyone had believed her baby was Matthew's. And that had been the final blow. Sure, they'd been corrected, but if Matthew's own family questioned them—questioned her—what chance did she have with anyone in town?

Annie replayed Marie's words through her mind. *It's what everyone will think.*

There was no escaping that truth. Not anymore.

* * *

Matthew ignored his mom's concerned expression. He'd walked on thin ice before. "Annie's going to nap for a bit."

"Babies tire a person out." Monica gave him a pointed look, along with two horseshoes. "You know that, right?"

Did she think he was stupid? He'd changed his share of Luke's diapers. Even Erin's. "You got something to say?"

"Maybe."

"Then say it." Matthew challenged.

"Monica, stop it." Their mom intervened.

"And you wonder why I've never brought anyone home before," he muttered.

His mom cuffed the back of his head. "Knock it off and play."

"Oww." He stepped into the sandpit and glared at his sister.

Monica stuck her tongue out.

"You're both soooo mature." Erin stood with arms folded at the opposite horseshoe pit. As Monica's partner, the two of them would get crushed like always. "Let's go."

Matthew threw his shoe. It hit the pole with a clang and bounced off. No points there.

Erin was only twenty-three and the baby sister. The one everyone had looked after and made sure stayed on the straight and narrow. Having six older brothers made it impossible for her to bring anyone home.

The last fellow had been the kid who'd picked her up for senior prom. Erin still hadn't forgiven Marcus and Ben for sticking a rotten fish in the backseat of the kid's car while it was parked during the dance.

Matthew had been the one elected to console her after the date ended too soon. He'd had to explain that their prank had more do to with keeping Erin out of trouble than anything else. Not the most comfortable conversation he'd had with a sister, but a necessary one.

He threw another shoe and it bounced on the ground and rolled away.

"Nice one." Luke was his partner and not very pleased with his shoe-tossing performance thus far.

"Get your head in the game," Monica ground out.

"What's with you?" He pushed her shoulder before she released her shoe, knocking off her aim.

She whirled on him. "Do that again, and you'll find out."

He laughed as he always did. Monica was four years his junior and the prickly one in the family.

Their mom rolled her eyes. "Do I have to separate you two?"

They'd heard that before, too. Millions of times. He and Monica had fought the most, but she was the sister he felt closest to. Maybe because of the scratchy exterior she hid behind. Monica might be twenty-eight and successful with a web design and marketing business, but she wasn't as confident as she portrayed. As the middle sister, Monica got lost between their sister Cat's achievements and Erin's easygoing sweetness.

Monica looked at him and grinned. Then she threw her second horseshoe and landed a ringer.

They played for half an hour, but Matthew and Luke couldn't manage a win. Beaten. By their sisters. The four of them exited the horseshoe lane to make way for the next two teams.

"That's it for us." Matthew wiped his hands on the front of his T-shirt.

"Too bad," Monica said.

Matthew nodded toward the fire. "I think I'll check on Annie."

Monica gave him a stern look. "So, what's the deal with all that?"

"Don't you like her?" Matthew couldn't imagine what reason Monica might have, but her expression was far from approving.

"My opinion has nothing to do with it."

He grinned. "Never stopped you before."

"Ha-ha. Seriously, though, isn't this a little fast? You weren't interested in settling down, and now you're ready to raise someone else's kid."

"Things change."

Monica shrugged and then gave him a gruff hug. "As long as you're happy, I'm happy."

"Same with me for you. The right guy's out there for you."

Monica's eyes grew stormy. "He's taking his sweet time!"

That sounded a lot like she had someone specific in mind. But before he could ask, Monica had moved out of conversation distance. He'd let it go for now. She wouldn't tell him, anyway.

Matthew looked around.

Darren and their dad against Cam and Marcus were the last two pairs to play. He'd seen this matchup many times before and could easily predict the outcome. No one beat Darren and Dad.

Walking toward the dying fire close to the sandy beach, he slipped into a chair next to Annie. Her eyes were closed and she rested folded hands across her middle. His shirt lay draped over her, and her thick hair tumbled around her shoulders.

She looked peaceful in sleep.

He felt anything but. Tomorrow morning he'd travel hours to catch ship for his next rotation. He wanted a future with Annie, but his mother's words nagged that it wasn't the right time to press that. Monica's concern with timing increased his doubts.

Was he pushing too hard?

Annie opened her eyes and stared at him. "Hey."

"This is getting to be a habit, watching you sleep." He chuckled. "Have a good nap?"

"Actually, I did." She sat up and yawned. "Where is everyone?"

He jerked his head toward the sound of clanging metal. "Still playing shoes."

She nodded and looked away, staring at the glowing embers of an old fire.

"What's wrong, Annie?"

She blew out her breath. "We need to talk."

True, but hearing her say it didn't sound good. He offered his hand. "Let's walk, then."

She took it and stood, then held out his shirt.

"You can wear it."

She slipped it on and folded her arms.

Even her body language didn't bode well. She was shutting him out. Self-protective because he was leaving or something more? He aimed to find out.

They walked the shoreline in silence, along a well-worn path.

"It's pretty here," Annie finally said.

"I think so." Matthew knew small talk when he heard it. Annie's attempt at inane chatter spoke volumes. Something bothered her.

Looking out over the small lake, he saw a kingfisher swoop down and nab a minnow. Frogs belched out their evening songs and a dog barked in the distance.

She stopped walking and looked up at him. "Your rotation came at a good time."

His gut tightened. "Why's that?"

"I think we need to call it quits for a while."

He narrowed his gaze. "Why?"

Annie rubbed her forehead. "I need to figure some things out. If we make a clean break, if we agree not to call each other, it'll give us both time to think things through, find out what we really want."

Matthew considered her request. It wasn't as if he had time or cell coverage to call her much, anyway, so there had to be more to it. "Annie, what's really bothering you?"

She took a deep breath. "I need time."

"Okay, I get that. When I get back we can—"

She held up her hand, stalling him. "I'm not talking about a couple of months. I'm talking about real time like well after the baby's born, after I settle into being a mom. Right now I need to focus on that. Expecting you to fill Jack's shoes isn't fair to either of us."

"What makes you think that's what you're doing?"

Annie shrugged. "I heard about the seagull on the *William Lee Block*. I saw the picture of you and the baby raccoon. Monica even admitted that you have a soft spot for orphans and widows."

His stomach churned fire. "You think this is about me feeling sorry for you?"

"Face it, Matthew. You feel responsible for me because you're the one who found Jack. Maybe deep down you feel guilty."

His guilt stemmed from feelings for her. Feelings he'd had for a long time now.

"Sure, I feel a level of obligation to Jack. But why is that a bad thing? We've known each other a long time.

It should be no surprise when our friendship turns into something deeper."

She struggled for composure, then stepped closer and cupped his face. "I'm not a young woman. I pray I'll have this child just fine, but there's a good chance this is it for me. There won't be any more."

He let that sink in. Jack's boy may be the only son he'd ever have. The only child. He hadn't given much thought to having a family because that limitation had never been a reality. At thirty-two, he had plenty of time. Annie, at forty, didn't.

He placed his hands on her hips and let his forehead fall to hers. "Something to consider, I suppose."

She pulled back. "Not having kids gnawed at Jack."

"I'm not Jack."

She faced him. "I know, but—"

He pulled her back to him. "Annie, look at me."

She did.

"I'm not Jack."

Then she lowered the boom with a shrill sound to her voice. "And that's part of the problem, don't you see?"

He didn't.

Her eyes filled with tears. "I'm pregnant and I need to honor Jack's memory. Alone."

"You are. We both are. How do we dishonor Jack by being together?"

She looked at him like he was an idiot for not following her. "Your family believed this baby was yours."

"After I put my foot in my mouth and said 'that's my boy.' They know the truth, Annie."

"But others don't and they won't. If we continue seeing each other, they'll always wonder."

Irritation ripped through him. "You care too much

what other people think. If the ones that count know the truth, what difference does it make?"

"It makes a big difference to me," she growled. "I won't have anyone question where my son comes from."

Once again, the gossip and whatever Jack's mom had said dogged her thoughts. He'd hoped meeting his family, especially his mom, might have trumped that. Obviously it hadn't. And he'd made things worse with his offhand remarks.

He searched her eyes. She cared more about what people might think of her than what they had. Maybe his mother was right. Annie wasn't ready for his love. Might never be ready.

"It's too soon," she whispered.

He'd really grown to hate that statement. "Says who?"

"Me." She lifted her chin.

Stubborn woman.

That wasn't true. If it was, she'd never have spent so much time with him. "So you're going to let what others think get in the way of something that might last a lifetime?"

"I have to, Matthew. I have a business to run." She sighed and walked away from him.

"But, I love you, Annie. I always have."

She whipped around, her face pale. "Don't say that."

He wanted to shake sense into her, tell her that breaking off all contact was yet another loss. An unnecessary one. "Did you ever wonder why there was never anyone else? No one compared to you."

She covered her ears. "Stop it! We were friends—I never wanted anything more!"

"I'm not blaming you. You didn't do anything wrong. You were simply being you, and I—"

"I love Jack—" Her voice cracked as tears ran down her flushed cheeks.

He reached for her.

"Don't."

He might be a navigational whiz on the lakes, but he'd never been good at emotional warning signs. He never should have admitted what he couldn't take back. Angry, because of her stubborn pride, Matthew had pushed ahead. Not fighting fair, he'd admitted his feelings before she'd been ready to hear them.

Watching Annie's spirit shrivel up and die was certainly no prize. Misplaced guilt was an ugly thing to behold.

"Annie, I'm sorry." He reached for her again.

She sidled away from him looking wary and afraid. "I think it's time I went home."

Chapter Thirteen

Annie wanted to be sick. Sitting in the passenger side of Matthew's truck, she stared out the window at the blazing sunset streaking across the sky in ribbons of orange and pink. It took effort to ignore the sweet scent of strawberry-rhubarb pie seeping out from under its plastic wrap making her already tense stomach coil tighter.

Had she encouraged Matthew somehow while Jack was alive? They'd always joked around, but had he taken that as something else? Memories flashed through her mind, but nothing struck her. Matthew had always made her laugh, but he'd never been anything but respectful toward her. He'd treated her like a friend—always a friend and nothing more.

How could he have *always* loved her?

An odd image suddenly sprang to life. Not so long ago, during the off-season when their freighter was laid up for winter, Matthew had stopped in to pick up Jack for something they'd planned to do.

While Jack was changing his clothes, Matthew joined her in the kitchen as usual. They had always chatted comfortably before, even without Jack right there, but that one time they were quiet. That morning there'd been a current of tension in the room that she'd shrugged off as her imagination.

"He cares for you. I think he always has."

Ginger had been right all along. That red letter sewn across her heart exploded back to life with a sharpness that took her breath away.

But she hadn't been attracted to Matthew until recently. She'd never wanted his attention before…

"I loved Jack, too, you know." Matthew's voice was soft and intruded on her thoughts.

"I know." She glanced at him.

"I'd never have come between the two of you. I'd have transferred and moved away before causing either of you trouble."

Her heart twisted. She missed her husband more than ever. What she wouldn't give for Jack's quiet assurance. His wisdom. She'd never been the clinging type, had never once bawled over Jack leaving, but tonight she might.

Over Matthew.

He had come between them. When Jack died, Matthew had stepped in. Her stomach turned again.

In the morning, Matthew would join his freighter in port and wouldn't be back for months. And then what?

If Ginger had seen through Matthew's feelings, had everyone else? She didn't want anyone ever doubting her love for Jack. But more so, she didn't want her son wondering if maybe the rumors had been true. Rumors that would stick if she didn't stay away from Matthew.

She closed her eyes.

"Annie, I have no right to ask, but I want you to do something for me."

Tears threatened to choke her, so she nodded.

"Please call my mom if you need anything. She's there for you, no matter what."

Annie nodded again.

"And pray. Ask God for direction. Not the opinion of Marie Marshall. Don't take what she says as gospel truth."

Annie shifted as they pulled into her driveway. If Matthew realized what he'd give up to be with her, he'd take this chance and run. She wouldn't blame him a bit if he did.

Matthew sighed. "I hate leaving like this."

"I know." Her doing. But it had to be done.

His gaze searched hers.

She had to get out or lose her resolve. Annie slipped to the ground from Matthew's truck, but waited. "This is for the best."

He didn't look convinced. "Maybe not."

She did her best to smile and failed. "Be careful, Matthew, and take care of yourself."

"You, too, Annie."

She closed the door and headed into her house. Their goodbye sounded so final. And that hurt, yet it felt right. As she flicked on a light, no other sound greeted her but the noise of Matthew's truck pulling away. He was gone.

She slid to the floor and cried.

Never before had she felt so alone.

The following morning, Annie drove toward Jack's parents' house. Traffic crept along even though it was Sunday, Father's Day. The campgrounds were already filling up with tourists. Several trucks with fifth wheels and campers pulled into the state park in front of her forcing her to slow down to a crawl. She wasn't in the mood and glanced in her rearview mirror at the line of cars behind her.

How far did Matthew have to drive to catch ship?

She shook her head, hoping to clear him from her thoughts. Breaking it off was right for everyone. In time, maybe...

A car horn blared, startling her to move ahead.

She stopped at the bakery on the way and picked up a coffee cake she knew her father-in-law loved. She couldn't leave things the way they were with Marie and wanted to announce her news to Jack's dad in person.

Taking a deep breath, she knocked on their front door. No answer. Jack's parents were early risers. Surely they hadn't left for the nine o'clock summer service at their church.

Annie knocked again.

The door opened and Marie's eyes widened. "Annie."

She plastered on a smile and raised the bakery box. "Can I come in?"

"Yes, of course." Marie stepped back. "We were just sitting down to breakfast. Have you had yours?"

"No." Annie wasn't sure she could eat anything.

"Then join us." Marie's voice sounded softer than normal.

"Maybe." Annie took a deep breath and entered.

She was here to make amends, so eating breakfast might have to be part of that. Leaving her purse by the door, she followed Marie into the kitchen. It had been a while since her last visit and her throat immediately tightened. Hadn't she'd cried enough already?

She set the bakery box on the table and cleared her throat. "Morning, John. Happy Father's Day."

His face brightened and he peeked inside. "You remembered."

"Of course." Annie slipped into a chair. The familiar scent of melted margarine and fried bacon wrapped around her. For once, it comforted rather than repulsed.

Jack's father was close to seventy. John Marshall had retired as a merchant marine captain years ago, but he kept tabs on freighters through an online website. He also tuned into life on the Great Lakes with a marine radio scanner.

Much to Marie's irritation, the scanner was on this morning, crackling to life with various mates and captains checking traffic conditions at the Soo.

"John, please turn that thing off," Marie said.

The deep lines in his weathered face crinkled as he winked at Annie. But he did what his wife told him and clicked off the radio. Then he smiled. "Marie tells me you have some special news."

Annie glanced at Marie, who nodded. John wanted to hear it from her. "You're going to be a grandpa come before Thanksgiving time."

John's smile widened even more and his eyes teared up. "Jack would be proud, and so am I."

Great, now I'm really going to cry.

"Thanks," Annie whispered.

"If you'll pray, we can eat." Marie set a platter of steaming eggs, bacon and hash browns on the table.

Jack's father bowed his head. "Lord, we thank You for this food, but we thank You even more for the gift of life. May we not take any gift from You for granted. Amen."

"Amen," Annie and Marie echoed in unison.

"Go ahead and dig in. You need to feed that baby." Marie patted her shoulder before sitting down across from her husband.

Annie stared at the grease-laden food. Marie fried her eggs in bacon grease. Jack had loved his mother's heavy breakfasts and had often complained that Annie wouldn't make them. She'd never been able to eat pork, and bacon grease didn't exist in her world. Funny, but all those healthy meals she'd forced on Jack hadn't helped him a bit in the end.

Annie scooped up one egg and a spoonful of potatoes. "Thanks."

"Coffee cake?" John had a cut a small slice that dripped with cherries, almonds and icing.

Annie lifted her plate to accept it. "Yes, please."

Marie smiled at her. *Actually smiled!*

Maybe what Matthew had said was true. Could Marie's harsh words have been more about her own hurt, than gospel truth? She peeked at the clock on the wall that read eight-thirty. Even if she missed her own church service at ten, Annie aimed to find out. But first, she'd have to choke down a greasy egg.

"Weather's been good," John said. "How's that garden of yours coming along?"

Annie forced a smile. The memory of Matthew tilling up the soil made her want to weep. "Just fine."

"What did you plant?" Marie asked.

Annie filled them in and then they fell into an awkward silence as they finished eating. Finally, Annie stood to help clear the table.

"I can take care of this if you need to leave." Marie headed for the sink.

She hesitated, dish in hand. "Do you want me to leave?"

Marie stared her down.

This time, Annie didn't flinch or look away. She simply stayed quiet and waited.

"No, Annie. I don't want you to leave."

"I'm going to fill the bird feeders." John gave his wife a pointed look.

The tension smoldered in the room.

Marie smoothed the front of her apron over and over. "Annie, about the other day, I may have jumped to the wrong conclusions…"

Annie wanted to scream out how much that had hurt. But then Marie hadn't been the only one who'd gone there. And Annie had needed a wake-up call.

"Matthew's gone on the lakes, but I broke it off."

Marie's eyes narrowed. She rinsed a dish and handed it to her. "Why?"

Annie wasn't used to sharing personal things with her mother-in-law. Placing the plate in the dishwasher's bottom rack, she thought about how to best answer the question and decided on the simple truth. It all boiled down to one thing. "I still love Jack."

Steam circled around Marie's arms as she rinsed another dish and handed it over. Her mother-in-law looked pleased but also sad. "You'll always love Jack. That won't go away. But I think you made a wise decision."

Annie thought so. But that didn't make it hurt any less. Time away was a good thing, but scary, too. Given time to step back and really think, Matthew might realize he wanted a family of his own and a wife young enough to give him one.

Chapter Fourteen

September

Matthew stood on deck. The dark waters of northern Lake Superior churned and a three-quarter moon illuminated the sky overhead along with a scatter of stars. The cool night air of early September chilled, but he didn't go inside. Not yet. He had forty-five minutes before he needed to report for his watch. At three in the morning, he should still be tucked into his warm bunk, asleep.

These days sleep never came quick during down time. His nagging conscience made sure of that. Thoughts of Annie tore at his waking hours, too. She hadn't been the one to betray Jack. He had. He'd fallen for Annie long before he'd admitted it. Even to himself.

Thou shalt not covet thy neighbor's wife.

His stomach pitched as it always did when he thought about breaking the tenth commandment. Oh, he'd made his peace with God and even Jack out here in the wee hours. But Matthew felt the need to lash his back a few times. And this morning was one of those times. He didn't deserve the forgiveness he knew he'd received.

Bozia punish.

His grandmother's saying—used by his mother, too—referenced God by the Polish term. Was God truly punishing him for his sin or was losing Annie the consequence of his own ill-timed actions? Whatever it was, by admitting his feelings too soon, he'd pushed Annie away.

Maybe for good.

"You're up early." Wyatt, their temporary captain, handed him a steaming cup of coffee.

Matthew took the cup with a grateful nod. "So are you."

Wyatt slapped him on the shoulder. "The older I get, the less sleep I need."

Matthew sipped the strong brew. "Thanks for this."

"You're welcome. Something eating at you?"

Matthew shrugged.

"Can't say when you'll get a reprieve. With your replacement laid up, I'm going to need you for a while yet."

"That's fine." He had no one to go home to.

Not that he had much choice in the matter, but if Annie wanted time apart, she'd have that and more. He'd abided by her no-call rule even though it killed him. There wasn't much more to say that hadn't been said, but he missed her voice. Her smile. Her.

"Good thing Annie Marshall knows the drill."

Matthew looked sharp at the captain. "What makes you say that?"

Wyatt rubbed his chin. "I heard the guys mention that you were seeing her. Makes sense. I understand you and Jack were pretty tight."

In his world, no one cared about their relationship. In Annie's, it seemed as if everyone cared too much. At least, Annie thought so. "I was just helping her through a rough time."

Wyatt looked at him closely. "Take some advice from an old man?"

Matthew hadn't asked, nor did he want it, but he smiled, anyway. "What's that?"

"Life's short. Folks dance around an opportunity too long and then it's gone."

"Right. Thanks." Matthew checked his watch. "I might as well check in."

Wyatt shook his head.

Matthew wasn't listening. Wouldn't listen. He hadn't waited and that's what got him in trouble. He'd tried to grab his opportunity too soon, before Annie was ready for it. His impatience had only heaped guilt on her. Guilt she had no business feeling. He'd fallen for who she was, not because of any encouragement on her part.

The only thing he could do now was wait and pray. He'd give Annie her space. He'd wait and hope she'd come to him when she was ready. No more pushing. And no more guilt.

God knew his contrite heart. And the desires locked safely therein. This time, he'd wait on God's mercy and grace to pave the way for him. He'd trust the time of punishment was past when Annie welcomed him back into her life.

"Phew! Done!" Ginger tossed the last paint brush into the bucket. "It looks really nice, too."

"I think so." Annie scanned the nursery and smiled.

They had painted the walls navy blue with screaming white trim. Even the wraparound shelf that John had made was bright white. And the perfect perch for Jack's model ship. Marie and John had even purchased the white crib and matching changing table.

"How about lunch on the back deck? I ordered from

your favorite—Bernelli's. We might as well enjoy this warmth while it lasts." Annie adjusted the fat clip that held her hair.

"Wow, thanks."

"No, thank you for helping me." Annie rubbed her growing belly when she heard the doorbell ring and headed for the stairs.

"I'm glad I can finally close the shop on Mondays and have two days off in a row like normal people." Ginger had chosen to spend her Sunday and Monday painting the nursery.

"I'm glad, too." After Annie got home from her Monday morning dance class, they'd gone to work. "It's nice when the summer people return to where they come from. My classes are back to regular year-rounders."

Annie opened the front door, paid for the food and tipped the delivery guy. "Thanks."

This year, Annie was more grateful than usual for the end of summer. With Matthew gone on the lakes, the juicy gossip about them had dried up to nothing. No more raised eyebrows. She was simply a pregnant widow who garnered sympathy and well wishes. She'd even picked up a couple new ballet students who were year-round residents.

Things had slowed into a new, more normal rhythm.

Ginger poured two glasses of iced tea and then they ambled out onto the deck and ate lunch.

Annie's heart pinched when she looked over her still-flourishing garden. September days had been warm, but the nights grew chilly. The leaves had started to turn announcing that fall was on its way.

"Have you heard from Matthew?"

"No. I don't expect to." Annie had hoped to go through the day without mentioning him. But then Ginger wouldn't leave the subject alone. In her opinion, Annie had made a mistake.

"Why don't you call him? You know you want to."

"I can't."

"Why not?"

"Because it's not right."

Ginger rolled her eyes. "This isn't the old days when a woman had to wear nothing but black and mourn for a year."

"Well, maybe it should be. Jack's memory deserves to be honored."

Ginger shook her head. "Don't you think he'd be glad about you and Matthew?"

"I don't know." She couldn't shake the guilt that came with knowing how Matthew felt about her. How she felt in return so soon after Jack's death.

Was that really *love*...

Annie had prayed, she'd counseled with her minister and she'd even joined an online support group of grieving widows and clarity still eluded. Several women who'd lost their husbands had confirmed her attraction to Matthew as a natural reaction to her loss. She simply missed her husband's attention and Matthew was the closest one to Jack.

Instead of helping, that common sense statement had condemned her even more.

"If this is real, then it will last." That was the mantra she went with, but it didn't stave off the worry that Ginger made a good point. "We simply have to wait it out."

Ginger shook her head. "Wait what out? The gossip? That's old news and who cares."

"I do." Annie grabbed a couple of wicker baskets that she kept in the laundry room.

"That sounds like pride talking."

"I'm not talking about this anymore." Annie glared at her friend. "Do you want to help me in the garden or not? Whatever you pick is yours."

"Absolutely." Ginger smiled without apology and then followed her off the deck and into the backyard.

In the garden, Annie had always found peace. Focused on the simple act of weeding, snipping back herbs or picking vegetables, she'd calm her thoughts. Today was no exception. Tomatoes were plump and red, the dill fragrant and her eggplant showed real promise in size.

"Hey, what's this?" Ginger pulled out a watch from the dirt and handed it over.

Touching the brown leather band, Annie felt her stomach drop. She struggled for composure.

"Oh, Annie, I'm sorry. Is it Jack's?"

Eyes burning and throat tight, she shook her head. "No. It's Matthew's."

Ginger's expression softened. "Love doesn't keep time. It's obvious you're in love with the man. Why torture yourselves because of preconceived notions of what's proper and expected?"

"I'm trying to do the right thing, especially for my son."

"So you wait a year or more and then what? Your son will grow up calling Matthew daddy, anyway. He'll have the Marshall name, so what difference does it make?"

Annie chewed her bottom lip. Ginger couldn't be right. Life wasn't that simple.

"Listen to your heart, Annie. That's where God speaks."

But her heart had been sewn up tight with red thread and red letters she didn't want seen.

She felt her cell phone vibrate inside the pocket of her sweats. "Hello?"

"Hi, Annie, it's Helen."

She glanced at Ginger. "What's up?"

"I just wanted to let you know that Matthew's going to be out on the lakes another month or two."

Her pulse skidded to a stop. She wouldn't be seeing him anytime soon. "Oh, okay."

A glimmer of hope flickered like a candle in a dark room. "Umm, did he ask you to call me?"

"No, honey, he didn't, but I thought you should know."

The glimmer flickered out and died. Matthew gave her exactly what she'd asked for—a clean break with no contact. He'd extended it, too. Maybe he had changed his mind about her, given time to think. Her wise decision felt more like payback.

"Thanks, Helen." Annie stuffed the phone back in her pocket.

"What's wrong?" Ginger stepped forward.

"That was Matthew's mom. He's working another rotation, probably another two months."

Ginger touched her arm. "Call him."

"No." Hearing his voice would only make things harder.

Most likely, Matthew didn't have a choice in remaining on ship. This summer's shipping season had been busier than normal. Even Jack's father had said so on one of her recent visits to drop off tomatoes.

No, she wouldn't call when her feelings were in turmoil. Maybe this was God's way of shutting that door and answering her prayers. Annie had to see this thing through and put Matthew out of her mind. Out of her heart.

And silently, she counted so she wouldn't cry.

But a small voice deep inside prayed that Matthew hadn't changed his mind.

Chapter Fifteen

October

Annie finally had it together. She missed Matthew, but every time she thought of him, she'd say a prayer. Positive doctor appointments and a baby shower at her church waved a big flag that the next few weeks would fly by. Her due date was less than three weeks away. This time the following month, she'd finally be a mom.

She stepped into the nursery and ran her fingers over the white rocking chair given to her from the Zelinsky family. Boy baby clothes, toys and a diaper pail were all in place.

Waiting.

All she did lately was wait.

Annie stared at the large model of a tall ship, the focal point of the room. "I think I've got this, Jack. I can do it."

You don't have to do it alone, Annie.

She sighed. She hadn't gone to the cemetery much lately. But she still talked to Jack. It comforted her, but then imagining how he might answer probably pushed it a little. "Your mom promised to help."

Not what I mean.

She didn't pretend that answer. It had come from out of nowhere. Wishful thinking maybe, but that whisper of her imagination felt different. Real even.

Listen to your heart. That's where God speaks.

She laughed out loud. Right. Maybe the closer she got to delivery, the more loopy she became. Hearing Jack's voice in her head and then pinning it on God.

Glancing at the clock, she carefully descended the stairs for yet another doctor's appointment. As she stepped out of the house, a cold wind tugged at her hair and plastered the warm knit material of her dress against her leggings. The temperature had dropped since this morning. She pulled her heavy cardigan sweater close and readjusted the woven scarf she'd wrapped around her neck.

Crunchy leaves swirled in the driveway while naked maple trees bent precariously low with another gust of wind. Even her neighbor's pumpkins seemed to shiver.

Sliding carefully behind the wheel, Annie started her car and pulled out. Not until she drove well out of Maple Springs did her heat kick in, but she felt the push of the wind against her small Honda with each mile.

The gales of November had come early. Where was the *William Lee Block*? Were they safe? Her doctor's office was near where Jack's parents lived. Maybe she'd stop in after her appointment and check with John.

The local highway followed the curve of the bay. Looking out over the water, she could see white caps and large swells. If conditions were this rough in a relatively protected bay, then how bad was it out in open water?

And then she saw the outline of a freighter on the horizon, and her heart skipped a few beats. It wasn't unheard of for ships to seek safe harbor in Maple Bay. It might be small, but it wasn't far from the shipping channel leading north through the Straits of Mackinac. Still, conditions must be bad to bring a massive bulk carrier in this far.

Annie grabbed her phone and hit the button for Marie's number.

"Hello?"

"Hi, Marie. I'm heading to my doctor's appointment, but can I stop by afterward?"

"Annie, is anything wrong?"

She swallowed hard. "Is John listening to his scanner?"

"Yes."

"I'd like to listen in, too." She wanted to know where Matthew's freighter might be on a day like this.

"Of course."

"Thanks, Marie." Annie disconnected.

Breathe, just breathe.

She'd been through this before. Gale-force winds were not uncommon on the lakes. Jack had ridden through some tough days and nights, but Annie hadn't always known about them. Maple Springs was nestled in a sheltered portion of the bay with its own tiny harbor. Despite the wind, calm waters remained there.

Early in their marriage, Annie had promised Jack that she wouldn't track his freighter. He'd asked her not to be one of those wives who'd call the company frequently, and she'd promised not to call unless absolutely necessary. Jack had always emailed her and then phoned when he put into port. She'd been good about keeping worry at bay.

But she'd asked Matthew not to contact her...

The parking lot of her doctor's office had a decent view of the bay and how it opened up into Lake Michigan. Nothing but gray skies, dark water and whitecaps. And that freighter.

"Dear Lord, please keep Matthew and his crew safe."

She repeated that prayer while waiting through her appointment. After receiving a good report and kudos on proper weight gain, Annie left the building, her thoughts on the weather. Dark clouds clustered along the western horizon of Lake Michigan. The freighter had anchored in Maple Bay and the silhouette of yet another laker loomed on the horizon.

When she pulled into the Marshalls' driveway, Marie opened the front door looking worried. "John's listening to the radio and it's not good."

Annie rushed into the kitchen where Jack's father sat hunched near the scanner. He had his laptop open on a site with an interactive map showing where on the Great Lakes named freighters and other ships were located.

She slipped into a chair next to him. "How current are those?"

"Says here it updates every fifteen minutes." John pointed at the screen.

"Where's the *Block*?" Matthew's bulk carrier.

"Last reported here, north of Green Bay Light." John clicked on a freighter marker shown and a pop-up of the *William Lee Block* came into view. In the picture, the freighter looked clean and sleek with its shiny black sides and gleaming white pilot house. Their destination was Rogers City, only a couple hours' drive away from Maple Springs.

When would they make it safely to port?

Gale-force wind warnings sounded from the scanner.

Annie shivered. "Why'd they leave Green Bay under these conditions?"

John didn't answer. What could he say? Deliveries had to be made.

"Have you heard from Matthew?" Marie asked.

"I asked him not to call me when he left in June." Annie chewed her bottom lip. *Stupid.*

Marie patted her back. "He'll be all right."

Not without Jack. Annie didn't know a thing about the temporary captain who'd hired on for this season. Matthew had mentioned that the guy was getting close to retirement age. Would he make the right calls? Or was he about getting one last fat bonus for keeping time in cargo delivered?

She spotted Jack's Bible, the one she'd given to his parents, lying open on the kitchen table. Her fingers itched to touch it. "May I?"

John flipped to a marked section and then pushed the leather-bound Word toward her. "Maybe you should see this."

Marie still looked worried. "John—"

"Let her be, Marie."

Annie had never heard Jack's father sound so stern. She glanced at Marie, but her mother-in-law had retreated to the sink with her back turned.

"See what?" Annie smoothed the pages that had been marked with sticky note tabs.

"I've been reading through Jack's scribbling throughout each book. Did you know he'd written so many notes in here?"

Annie nodded. It's why she'd given it to them. Jack hadn't merely read the Bible, he'd studied it.

John pointed. "Read that. Read it aloud."

She pulled the Bible closer and peered at the book of Deuteronomy, chapter twenty-five. "'When men have a dispute…'"

"Down some. Start at verse five."

"'If brothers are living together and one of them dies without a son, his widow must not marry outside the family. Her husband's brother shall take her and marry her and fulfill the duty of a brother-in-law to her…'" Annie's voice trailed off when she spotted Matthew's name in the margin.

You don't have to do this alone.

Her breath caught and she looked at John. "Did you write that?"

"No, Annie. That notation didn't come from me."

She ran her fingers over the penciled letters followed by a question mark. She shivered and wrapped her arms around herself to stop shaking. "You could have erased it."

John glanced at Marie's back, giving it away that his wife had probably suggested that very thing. "Jack once told me he loved Matthew like the brother he never had. Pretty clear to me that he wanted Matthew to take care of you if anything happened to him. Don't you think?"

Another tremor ripped through her. When had Jack penciled that in? Surely he hadn't known anything was wrong with his heart. He would have told her, wouldn't he?

Had Jack ever suspected Matthew's feelings for her?

Annie knew her husband, and Jack had been secure in their relationship. He'd known she'd loved him completely. She'd always love him, but Jack would want her free to love another.

But not just anyone.

Annie kept reading, silently. "The first son she bears shall carry on the name of the dead brother so that his name will not be blotted out from Israel."

It was Jack's voice she heard reading the passage. The only man Jack would ever trust raising their son was Matthew. That truth resonated deep in her heart. The heart she feared giving away because of the tattles from a few.

Annie had thought it noble and right to protect her reputation. Her image and her livelihood. But as Ginger had said, that was pride talking. Pure pride.

Her vision blurred and a tear drop fell on the open pages. She closed her eyes and felt her father-in-law's hand cover hers.

Then Marie sat down and pulled her into an awkward hug. "Call him, Annie. It's okay. See, even Jack said it's okay."

Annie lost it then. Sobbing, she hung on tight to Marie. Drawing quiet strength and even approval where she'd never expected it before.

Annie didn't let go. She'd never let go of Jack's blessing or his parents. Through better and worse, they'd become a family. A real family drawn closer by the gift of Jack's son.

Pacing John and Marie's plush dining room rug, Annie tried Matthew's cell phone number and got his voice mail.

"Matthew, it's Annie. There's nothing wrong, I'm fine, but I'm worried about you. Are you safe? Call me when you can."

Jack's parents lived in a modest home within a subdivision perched atop a hill with great views of Lake Michigan. Staring out the dining room window, Annie watched the waves on the bay. Two freighters were now anchored there, waiting out the storm.

Tapping the face of her phone, she called Matthew's mom.

"Hello?"

"Helen, it's Annie. Have you heard from Matthew?"

The woman chuckled. "I just got off the phone with him. They're heading for safe harbor. He didn't say where but wanted me to tell you that he'll call once they're anchored."

"Oh, good. Good." Annie pulled out a chair and sat down before her knees gave out.

"Are you okay? I can come over and wait with you."

Annie smiled. It was no wonder Matthew took care of orphans and widows. He'd had a good teacher. "I'm at John and Marie's."

"How's that working out?" Helen whispered as if Marie might hear.

The two women had met at Annie's baby shower at the church. An awkward introduction, but at least Marie hadn't snubbed Matthew's mom.

Annie let loose a nervous laugh. "Really well. In fact, they helped me see that I might have made a mistake breaking it off with your son."

Helen cooed. "You weren't ready. That's all."

Annie swallowed her pride and burst through those guilty stitches sewn across her heart. "I think I might be ready now."

"I'm glad. Welcome to the family, Annie."

"It's good to have family. Yours and Jack's."

"Always. Call me if you need me, honey."

Annie disconnected but didn't move. Gazing out the window without focusing, she fretted. When would Matthew call? When would she know that he was safe?

Her phone whistled, announcing a text.

From Matthew.

We're anchoring south of Escanaba. If there's room. I'll call soon.

She read the message over again. Surely he was joking about room. How rough was it out there? Rough enough to bring two freighters into Maple Bay. And that hadn't happened in years.

Annie closed her eyes and prayed again for the safety of the *William Lee Block*.

And she prayed for Matthew. "Please, God. Bring him home to me."

Matthew selected Annie's number and waited for her to pick up.

"Hello?" Her voice sounded low and sweet.

He'd called yesterday after they'd anchored to wait out the wind. But their connection had been poor and they weren't able to talk long. Weren't really able to talk at all. So he told her not to worry, they were fine, and promised to call again in the morning, once they made port.

That was hours ago. He had a better idea, made possible by his relief mate taking over.

"Morning, sunshine."

"Matthew?"

"Expecting someone else?"

"This connection sounds so clear. Where are you?"

He smiled. "What's the weather like there?"

She paused. "Ah, gray clouds, gloomy and cold. I think it's going to rain."

"Maybe you should go outside and check."

"I can see from the kitchen window."

"Try your front porch. I think it might be sunny there."

He heard her laugh, deep and rich sounding. "Where are you?"

He saw the dining room curtains pulled aside and her beautiful face break into a wide smile. Yup, pure sunshine.

Then she opened the door.

For a second, Matthew was stunned by the change

in her, unsure what to do next. Her protruding belly announced that it wouldn't be long before the baby came. Not long at all. Thanksgiving was a month away and she was due before that. But he'd be there if she wanted him to be.

She still managed to look beautiful dressed in black leggings and a long gray sweater. Her blond hair tumbled over her shoulders. Waves of more sunshine.

He pocketed his phone. Never once looking away from her, he walked up the sidewalk onto the porch steps and stopped.

Her eyes had filled with tears, but she still hadn't said a word. Her left hand covered her mouth. Her very bare left hand. She'd taken off Jack's ring.

He finally broke the ice by giving her a limp bouquet of fall-colored flowers that he'd picked up at a convenience store. "These are for you."

"Oh, Matthew." She closed the distance fast and wrapped her arms around him. "I'm so sorry."

He pulled her as close as he could, but her hard belly got in the way. "Don't be."

She pulled back and looked up into his eyes. "I was wrong. I was—"

He laid a finger against her lips. "It's okay. I can wait until you're ready, and I'm not going to change my mind. I love you, Annie. Always and forever. One baby or five, I'm with you. You're my soul mate, my first mate and I'd like to be your second husband. But it's your timetable. There's no hurry."

Tears ran down her cheeks and she smiled. "I love you."

That's all he needed to hear.

He lowered his face to hers and kissed her.

Deeply and thoroughly, she kissed him back.

And this time it was a kiss of certainty and assurance. A promise of their life ahead. Together.

Epilogue

December

New Year's Eve, Annie rocked her son to sleep near the fireplace. Her gift of a second rocking chair had come from Matthew. It was a gorgeous mission-style oak piece complete with a leather cushion that he'd found at an antique shop in town.

John Anthony Marshall III had been born the weekend before Thanksgiving. With Marie at her side. Matthew had agreed to exit the labor room with everyone else when it came time to push.

"How's our little man?" Helen smiled.

"Finally asleep." Annie snuggled her precious bundle closer and kissed the baby's forehead. "Matthew called, he should be here soon."

His mom nodded. "Good. I hate it when he's out on the lakes in this kind of blustery weather. I'm glad they're laying up early this year."

"Dinner's almost ready," Marie called from the kitchen.

Helen squeezed Annie's shoulder. "You sit tight. I'll set the table."

"Thanks." Annie continued to rock the baby.

John and Andy watched college football on TV. A fire snapped and crackled in the faireplace and her Christmas tree still twinkled with fresh life. Ginger had brought her a fresh-cut tree and then had helped her decorate it a few days before Christmas.

Her first Christmas home without Jack. Even Matthew had been gone, but she hadn't been alone. She and Little John spent Christmas Eve dinner at Andy and Helen's and then Christmas Day, John and Marie had brought dinner. The first of many holidays her son would share with his grandparents.

Both the Marshalls and Zelinskys.

Only one person had been missing. Matthew. But maybe that had been God's timing, too. Annie wanted to wake up with her son at home, instead of over at Helen and Andy's. Christmas morning, Annie had honored Jack's memory while feeding their son. Talking to him like she used to, filling Jack in on all that had changed. Especially his mother's heart. And even her own. Things were different between them.

She heard the front door open and the stamp of big feet.

Matthew.

A few moments later, he came through her tiny foyer into the living room wearing a silly Santa hat with an attached felt beard. Over his shoulder, he carried a big plastic garbage bag like a sack. "Ho, Ho, Ho. Merry Christmas."

"Shhhh, Matthew. The baby is sleeping," Helen scolded.

The baby startled awake but didn't cry. His eyes grew wide.

Matthew peered over her shoulder at him. "Hi, big guy."

Little John smiled. A wide, toothless, happy-to-see-you kind of smile that made Annie's eyes water.

"He knows me." Matthew's eyes looked a little bright, too.

Annie lifted her face. "Either that or he's a good friend of Santa's."

Matthew kissed her quick. "I missed you."

"Me, too."

"Hi, Matthew." Marie stood in the doorway, wiping her hands against her apron. "Perfect timing. Dinner's nearly ready. I made pot roast."

Matthew grinned. "Can't wait. That's my favorite."

"I know." Marie smiled back.

And Annie's heart swelled to bursting with thankfulness. So many things had changed since the sadness of spring. Even though she still missed Jack—they all did—she felt his blessing over such a gathering. God had doused them with the oil of joy and brought them out of the darkness of Jack's death.

Annie had been given a healthy baby boy born with a thatch of dark hair who drew two families together. Jack's son banished John and Marie's despair. Little John would grow up surrounded by love and fond memories of his father. Matthew had promised that. Something John and Marie appreciated.

Annie got up and shifted the baby.

While the grandparents headed for the washroom or kitchen to load the table, Matthew stalled her with a soft touch to her arm. "I have something for you."

She gave a pointed look at the bag he'd dropped by the tree. Boxes poked through the sides and Christmas wrapping paper patterns showed from underneath. "Don't you want to wait until later?"

He pulled a small black velvet-covered box out of his pocket. "Not for this."

She stared at it and her heart pounded.

"I thought we should make it official." He opened the box to reveal a ring of white gold with a gorgeous pearl set between two diamonds. "Marry me, Annie."

She looked at the beautiful ring that was so unique and yet held such meaning. The purity of the pearl resonated deep within her. They'd keep God in the center of their marriage.

Annie shifted her son and held out her hand. "Yes, Matthew. I will marry you."

He wrapped his arms around her, enveloping both her and Jack's son. "Happy New Year."

She smiled and kissed him. Sealing the promise of a better year ahead.

Annie couldn't help but also think of that pearl as a reminder of her precious gift from God. She had a son.

* * * * *

Dear Reader,

Thank you so much for picking up a copy of my book. I hope you enjoyed the first of several involving the Zelinsky family and their hometown of Maple Springs, Michigan.

Matthew and Annie are two characters who've been with me a long time, waiting quietly in my *idea file* for a chance to tell their story. I was intrigued by the concept of true love growing out of shared grief. And the obstacles they'd face in the process.

I think what Matthew and Annie went through can be relevant to any dark happening in our lives. If we shut out the chatter around us and focus our attention on God, seeking His wisdom, blessings can and will be found.

Many Blessings to you,
Jenna

I love to hear from readers. Please visit my website at www.jennamindel.com or drop me a note c/o Love Inspired Books, 233 Broadway, Suite 1001, New York, NY 10279.

REQUEST YOUR FREE BOOKS!

2 FREE INSPIRATIONAL NOVELS
PLUS 2
FREE
MYSTERY GIFTS

Love Inspired®

LI15

Love Inspired

JUST CAN'T GET ENOUGH OF INSPIRATIONAL ROMANCE?

Join our social communities
and talk to us online!
You will have access to the latest
news on upcoming titles and special
promotions, but most important,
you can talk to other fans about your
favorite Love Inspired® reads.

 www.Facebook.com/LoveInspiredBooks

www.Twitter.com/LoveInspiredBks

Harlequin.com/Community

LISOCIAL

Jenna Mindel lives in northwest Michigan with her husband and their three dogs. She enjoys a career in banking that has spanned over twenty-five years and several positions, but writing is her passion. A 2006 Romance Writers of America RITA® Award finalist, Jenna has answered her heart's call to write inspirational romances set near the Great Lakes.

Books by Jenna Mindel

Love Inspired

Maple Springs

Falling for the Mom-to-Be

Mending Fences
Season of Dreams
Courting Hope
Season of Redemption
The Deputy's New Family
His Montana Homecoming

"You don't have to worry about me, you know."

"I know." So why was he? Matthew thought about her a lot. Maybe too much. "But we both have to eat."

She smiled. "I am hungry. Let me throw on a cover-up and we'll go."

"I'll be right here." He meant it, too. She could lean on him. "Always here for you. I hope you know that."

This felt a lot like a date. Was he trying to date Annie Marshall? Surely, it was too soon to go there.

He glanced at the woman walking beside him. She was a few years older than him. Not that it mattered. Not to him. She'd always been beautiful.

Annie caught him staring. "What?"

"Nothing." He really needed to cover this awkward awareness or they'd have an uncomfortable dinner together. "I was just picturing your feet."

She rolled her eyes. "Real nice."

It felt good to tease her. As if they were friends again and nothing had happened to change that. There was no reason to let one kiss change what they were. They were friends. He needed to remember that.